HAU. SEWANEE

Annie Armour

HAUNTED SEWANEE
By Annie Armour

Copyright 2017

ISBN-13: 978-1548832445
ISBN-10: 1548832448
Softcover

On the cover: University Cemetery, Sewanee, TN
Photograph by Annie Armour

Dedication

To Janet, Sarah, and Meg just because they are the best.

Acknowledgments

First, I would like to thank the many people who gave me their stories to tell. Without them there would certainly be no book. I appreciate you more than you know.

Next, I am grateful to my daughters and others for keeping up the encouragement during the times I tried to forget I was writing a book. The times were many that they persevered for me.

Finally, I thank my husband, Chuck Morgret, for his editing skills and for navigating the actual publishing process. His help was invaluable.

Contents

The Headless Gownsman

Introduction

Sewanee is a small college town on the Cumberland Plateau in Southern Middle Tennessee. It is home to Sewanee: The University of the South, which includes a liberal arts school for about 1800 students, an Episcopal seminary, and a couple of Masters programs. Otherwise, it is a one-gas-station kind of town. When the students are gone, the population is cut by more than half. Granted, you can find plenty to eat with its ten dining establishments. There is a grand inn, a bookstore, and even a movie theater, but you won't find a clothing store or franchise of any kind, and the closest mall is 50 miles away. You have to love small town living to stay here.

Why, then, is there such a preponderance of ghosts in the area? Let me tell you how I found out about some of them.

I served as University Archivist from 1985 until my retirement in 2013. In that capacity, several years ago I was going to host a Halloween party at the Archives. A portion of the Archives had just been moved into a beautiful new space, a renovated fraternity house, and I wanted to show it off. The plan was to invite local kids to trick or treat early on, and tell ghost stories to college students later.

It was at that point that I realized I didn't really know any Sewanee ghost stories. There were four or five that had evolved over the years, but that was it. None of them sounded remotely believable, either. I spread the word over student and staff electronic networks hoping for a couple of first-hand stories to add to the repertoire.

I never dreamed I would receive so many! Besides students, faculty, and staff, alums began writing with ghostly tales on campus. Community members submitted them, too. In no time I had forty or more stories. Sewanee appeared to be more haunted than anyone thought. I created a Facebook group and collected even more stories there.

The day of the party ended up being rainy and chilly. People came to the Archives and stayed to avoid the miserable weather.

1

We had plenty to eat and drink. I started casually talking about ghost stories with our guests.

A young mother was there with her son. She told me, "I am a custodian at the University. I don't like to work at McCrady Dorm. I have seen the ghost of a young woman with brown hair and a purple dress there. She will be standing there and then suddenly disappear."

I could not believe it. The first story I had received after asking for ghost tales was one from a woman who had lived in McCrady Dorm in the 1970's. She described the very same woman! I was hearing virtually the same story from a person who had experienced it thirty years later. That story got me thinking about writing a book.

Every community seems to have a resident ghost or two, and some even a few more. Sewanee is teeming with them. I have collected stories on over seventy places (over 50 of them on University property) to date. Several dorms in particular have multiple stories associated with them over a span of time. Every time I tell stories, I get more in return. I decided I had better get this book written because if I waited to get all the possible stories, I would never finish.

This book is only a beginning. When you are walking across campus on a foggy evening, or studying alone in the middle of the night, or even working during the day, you may encounter a Sewanee spirit of your own. It appears that lots of people just don't want to leave this place, and they don't! It is time for Sewanee to take its place among the most haunted communities in the U.S.

Being an Archivist, I had to slip a little history in about most of the haunted spots. Here's hope that you will become more familiar with Sewanee the place as well as Sewanee the haunted haven.

Nearly all the names of people mentioned in the stories have been changed!

Academic Buildings

All Saints Chapel

A chapel's no place for a ghost
But All Saints had one who played host.
His music for all
Was heard in the hall
Until lights made him flee from his post.

The eyes and ears of All Saints' Chapel have seen and heard much since 1905 when it was first built. The first phase of construction left it with a wooden roof and no clerestory windows or bell tower. The University's museum flags hung over the congregation, and a large religious art piece painted by the University's first artist-in-residence, Johannes Oertel, adorned the wall above the altar. Chapel was held twice daily and everyone was welcome, including dogs. It was never locked, so one could roam through it for inspiration, prayer, mischief, curiosity, organ practice, or any other reason day or night.

The Ghost of the Organ in the Chapel

Stuart was living in the dormitory then called the "Sewanee Inn" (now Elliott Hall) from 1950 to 1952. One evening his friend Ned came in rather bug-eyed after having been at work late with Joe in the chemistry lab in the old science building (Carnegie – now used for Photography, Art History, Astronomy, and Administrative purposes) which is located in the middle of the quadrangle. For some reason Stuart was in the Elliott Hall lobby, so Ned related his story to Stuart.

It was about midnight when Ned and Joe left the lab. As they passed the chapel they heard magnificent organ music being played. At that time the chapel had a direct control tracker organ located on the left in the chancel just behind the first choir stalls, and it was never locked.

They decided to go in and see who was playing such beautiful music so late at night. They entered quietly by the main entrance on the west end of the chapel. They walked quietly up the aisle. The loud organ would have covered any sound that they might have made. There were no lights on, and no lights on at the organ. When they were at the crossing Ned, being a sacristan, quietly stole to the sacristy (to the left) where the switches were... to turn on the lights. Joe waited at the crossing until the lights came on as the music continued.

The lights came on. The music stopped. There was no one on the organ bench and there was no rustling or bumping noise of someone trying to get away. Ned entered the choir area from the altar rail steps and Joe went up into the choir from the crossing. No one was in the chapel.

There were stories of "the ghost of the organ" that had circulated before in Sewanee. It was supposed to be the ghost of a talented seminarian from some years before who had died tragically. He still made his presence known from time to time, mainly playing beautiful music on the chapel's organ.

When the new chapel was completed in 1959 the old tracker organ was replaced with a larger and more fitting one for the present building. The organ was moved to one of the side balconies in Guerry Hall, site of the stage for the performing arts at the time and still a venue for music, dance, and other productions. There are rumors from the 60's and 70's that a ghost made music on that organ when it was in Guerry. Eventually the organ was sold and moved off campus. Whether the ghost moved with the organ, stayed in Guerry, moved back to All Saints, or vanished is not known, but he has not been heard playing the current organ in the chapel.

Career Services

The current Career Services house has had two previous owners – Dean George Merrick Baker and the Hatchett family. Neither of those owners and none of the Career Services staff has ever reported a ghost here, but during the brief time the house served as the Russian House, I had a report of something very evil up in the attic area. Susanna, a former student who also happened to work for me in the Archives, came in one day a little frantic from the weekend. She had moved temporarily to the Russian house and was unofficially staying in an empty room in the attic. (This room later served as retired English professor Willie Cocke's office, and he never had a spooky moment in that room. Now it is just an attic.)

Susanna came home one night after a party and went upstairs to go to sleep. Some time later she was awakened by a noise, only to find a huge black apparition standing at the foot of her bed. He spoke to her, though it may not have been in words. "I am going to kill you!" The figure moved closer to her and covered her nose and mouth. She struggled and got out of it. The ghost continued to threaten her, getting larger and hovering over her, and at times moving away, and she had to focus on him to keep him at bay. Finally, she suddenly woke up and realized that when she had fallen asleep the ghost left.

Did she dream it? Was it a hallucination? It was still very real to her several days later!

There is another story about this site, when it held the University's first boarding house, Tremlett Hall. The house faced what is now University Avenue, but was large enough to encompass some of this property as well. This story was written for the 1910 *Purple*, the student newspaper, and is not a true story, but is a great read:

The Old South Room
by Stephen F. Austin, '10

Having finished classes early this morning, for it was my easy day, I sat smoking a meditative pipe on the dormitory steps, when it suddenly occurred to me that I had not seen Bill Doroughty at chapel that morning. Thinking perhaps he was sick, I sauntered over to the old ramshackle building, where some of the students, Doroughty among them, preferred to stay, rather than in the main dormitory for the ostensible reason that, being quieter, it afforded them a better opportunity to study ~ really because there they came under the less direct supervision of the proctors.

Doroughty was a great husky fellow something over six feet, an athlete to the core, and 'though he was a Freshman and I a Senior, I took a great interest in him partly because he was a frat brother of mine, and partly, yes, I confess it, because his sister was coming up for Commencement – now only a few weeks off.

I knocked at the door.

"Go to the Devil!" came from behind the panels in a lusty voice, "I'm sick."

This was Doroughty's way of extending a most cordial invitation to enter. Consequently I pushed the door open and walked in. He was sitting in a huge chair, with his back to the door, smoking moodily.

"Sick," I queried.

"Sure." he answered cheerily without turning round, "tonsillitis, dyspepsia and pleurisy, not to mention measles, tuberculosis, and whooping-cough. Doctor says I can't possibly live." He struck a match with great deliberation.

"Have a seat," he exclaimed when this delicate operation was satisfactorily accomplished, then turning towards me for the first time he cried, with the superb impudence of which only a Freshman is capable. "Why it's the Gownsman – the Headless Gownsman. Howdy?" and with this he kicked me a chair.

We sat discussing various subjects for a while. Finally Doroughty paused as though he had forgotten something, and thrusting his hand in the pocket of his dressing gown produced a crumpled bit of paper.

"Say Steve," he said, assuming a more serious air, "what do you make of this?" I took the paper and unfolded it. There were only two words written in a large uneven scrawl, such as a child might make, on it. They were, "Devil's Hole." My face must have shown my perplexity. "Make of it?" I said with a hearty laugh, "why – nothing." But Doroughty's face was so serious I checked my mirth. "What's the matter, old horse?" I asked, "Where did you get it?"

He did not answer immediately, but sat gazing at the scrap of paper in my hand, with a troubled expression.

"Oh," he exclaimed, finally, it's some brilliant Soph's trick," and the old good-humored smile returned to his face. But my curiosity was aroused. "Where did it come from," I insisted.

"Oh!" he returned with a laugh, "I've found one lying about every Friday morning, since I came over here in December. Pretty persistent, eh?"

I did not answer for my mind was busy trying to recall some scrap of conversation I had heard a short while before. Just then the dinner bell rang. Doroughty reached for his coat, "Oh, I forgot, "he said, "I'm sick. Have my dinner brought to me."

"All right," I answered.

As I was going out the door, however, he stopped me again. "Say, where is this 'Devil's Hole,' anyway," he asked.

"Out on the side of the Mountain under Morgan's Steep," I answered, "haven't you ever been there?"

"No," he snapped, "or I wouldn't have asked."

"Fair enough," I answered amiably, "go."

"Believe I will," he returned, "I'm curious."

After dinner I interviewed the matron.

"Mrs. Burk," I asked, "Who was the last man who stayed in the old south room at Tremlett?"

She looked at me curiously, "It's been unoccupied since 1906," she returned, "John Morris was the last who roomed there, poor fellow."

Morris - that was the name I had been trying to recall. I remembered it well enough now. Morris was a Senior during my Freshman year, but for some reason had disappeared, gone home we imagined, just before Commencement, without taking his degree. It had occasioned considerable comment at the time, but that Morris was a peculiar fellow, most of us thought a trifle out in the head, and the matter had soon dropped.

For the next week I had little time to think about the strange notes or the old south room, for examinations were drawing close and I was up for my degree. As for Doroughty, the whole affair seemed to have escaped his mind. He was convinced that some Sophomore was trying to worry him, and consequently gave the matter not another thought.

One Thursday night, however, I happened to be up pretty late. Before turning in, however, I suddenly remembered some letters to be posted, and so slipping on my coat I walked down to the mailbox some hundred yards from the dormitory. Returning I noticed a light in Doroughty's room. Knowing my friend to be no student, I was a bit surprised that he should be up at this hour, for it was nearing two o'clock. I crossed the campus and knocked at the door.

"Come in." he called.

He was lolling back in his Morris chair, smoking thoughtfully.

"Hello Steve," he said cheerfully, "sit down."

"What's up," I asked.

"Oh, I'm waiting for that scurvy Soph, " he returned. "If he'd been satisfied with writing notes, fair enough, but he's been doing the shoplifting stunt around here lately. Seems to be particularly fond of my brand of cigarettes and tobacco."

"Better put out the light if you want to catch him," I suggested, "or he'll know you are up."

"Hump, I never thought of that," said Doroughty, and he walked and blew out the lamp.

We sat smoking for perhaps a quarter of an hour, when suddenly I thought I detected a sound at the door that led out to the porch.

"Hush," I whispered, "here's our man."

Doroughty did not answer, but I heard him reach for the poker.

The fumbling at the door lasted only a moment, then I distinctly heard the latch shoot back. An instant later the door swung open revealing a square of starlit sky, against which was clearly silhouetted the mountain pine that grew in the middle of the path. Then it shut again with a sharp click.

I gave vent to a half-startled laugh. "The wind," I remarked lamely, but Doroughty did not

11

answer. Presently, however, he arose with a soft oath. "Steve," he said, "I could have sworn somebody opened that door, and yet, no one came in."

"Nonsense!" I exclaimed with a lightness I was far from feeling, "it was the wind."

"Curse the luck," he exclaimed, "I can't find the matches. Got one?"

"No." I answered, and then subduing my nervousness, "Don't light the lamp, we won't catch our man."

"All right," he said, and I heard him sink back in his chair. Presently, however, I saw a match drawn across the mantelpiece not three feet from where I sat. As it flared up I saw it applied to the end of a cigarette, and then tossed carelessly into the grate. It struck me as being particularly strange for I could have sworn Doroughty was on the other side of the room. Then I heard my friend's voice, peevish with impatience, "I thought you didn't have a match, tight-wad."

I was so taken aback by this statement that I sat for some seconds gazing at the burning coal as it periodically rose, glowed, and fell in the darkness.

Presently, however, I recovered from my surprise.

"But," I cried, springing forward, "here's our man," and reaching out, I seized the black shadow that seemed to loom before me. God! Shall I ever experience such another sensation? My hands closed upon something cold and slimy that yielded in my grip. Terrified, I sprang back, but the thing was upon me twining about me its soft stretchy arms that I could not evade nor tear loose with all my strength. Round and round the room we reeled in the dark – that cold, dead thing and I, fighting, kicking, tumbling over the broken chairs and tales – and ever that cigarette tip glowed steadily before my eyes. Finally I felt my strength leaving me. "Doroughty," I cried, with a last effort, "Doroughty, help" – and then my head must have struck against something for I lost consciousness.

When I awoke the day was just peeping through the windows. I tried to get up but I fell back with a groan, only to lose consciousness again. And then, it seemed to me that ages afterwards, I again come to myself - in the hospital ward this time, with my mother and sister bending over me.

And what became of Doroughty? Well - they found the poor fellow the next day, down under Morgan's Steep, grinning and jabbering like a mad man. His hair was streaked with gray and on his neck and wrists were great blue bruises, five of them all parallel, as though someone had beaten the flesh with a club. For several months he hovered between life and death - and then in the early fall the poor fellow passed away without telling the story of his awful experience.

Well no ~ we never explored "Devil's Hole" and now there is a great slab of rock over its mouth, put there at the order of the Trustees of the University. The old south room, too, has been torn down to make place for the handsome dormitory that now occupies the site of old Tremlett.

Well, that's about all. If you are looking for a moral in this story you will be disappointed. It simply happened.

(Story from *"The Sewanee Purple"* newspaper, 1910)

DuPont Library

There used to be a popular boarding house on the corner of Georgia Avenue and the former Alabama Avenue. It was named after its proprietress, Miss Van Ness. Eventually it became an apartment house for staff. It was taken down in the 1960's to make way for DuPont Library, and more than a few of the many people who lived there have commented that it was time for the old house to go.

When the library moved in 1965 from Convocation Hall to the new building, the campus community made a human chain and passed all the books from one building to the other. After 50 years the building is still timeless in its beauty with its solid oak wainscoting in open areas, towering two story windows in the reading room, brass handrails, and state-of-the-art music listening room.

In the Fall of 2008, a sophomore was in the library looking for a book for one of her classes. It was the early evening of the Thursday right after classes started. Often during the summer the library staff moves all the books to accommodate new arrivals, so when students come back in the fall, their favorite books are a few rows away from where they were the year before or even moved to a completely different floor. It always causes a bit of confusion. This student had to go to the second floor behind the main elevator and peruse the shelves for a bit.

14

The library is a dead place on Thursday evenings, particularly at the beginning of the school year. Upper class students typically find Thursday an excellent evening for socializing, and freshmen always have an orientation activity to attend at the beginning of the year. This student was pretty much the only student in the library at the time, and certainly the only one on the second floor, which is full of study carrels and faculty offices and not too many books.

She was looking for a particular book when all of a sudden she got the creepiest feeling that someone was watching her from behind the next row of books. All of her hair stood up on her arms and she got goose bumps. She tried to ignore the feeling at first because she really needed to find this book. It didn't usually take much time to do that, but all the books were shifted. It was a little annoying to be taking this long to begin with. After going down the next row of books, she got too spooked to keep looking. It felt as if someone was following her around through the shelves, and looking at her through the books. She tried in vain to see if someone was close by. Nobody. After a couple of minutes of this eerie feeling, she had to leave, and she didn't feel safe until she was downstairs by the front desk.

Her study carrel her freshman year was located close to where this occurred, and she never had any sensation like that before, even though she had been up there alone plenty of times in the past.

Although she never saw or heard anything that night or felt anything since, she has been a little unnerved by that area behind the elevator in the second floor since then, and feels weird going up there if there aren't a lot of people around.

Up until this story, the only hair-raising event at the library happened in the 70's when students took to streaking the library on a regular basis. This unnerved quite a few people.

Author's Note

One of my student assistants swears that on two occasions she saw Bishop Gailor wandering around in the back room of the Archives (when Archives was located in the library), a room that is dark and scary enough all by itself.

Not long before the Archives moved out of the library Shelley went into the restroom on the third floor at half past four to find the hot water turned on full blast. She had run into this several times over the year, though not usually the hot water. She always figured that someone was even more absent-minded than she was to turn a faucet on full blast and then leave it on. The next afternoon she went in again at half past four to find the faucet running again. The third day she deliberately checked the bathroom at half past four and found the faucet on yet again. She went around the whole third floor and asked the one student on that floor if she had used the restroom lately. She thought Shelley was crazy! Of course she hadn't been in there. That is not proof of a ghost, but it isn't proof that there isn't one, either.

Fulford Hall

Fulford Hall is a beautiful, huge, Victorian home that now houses the Offices of Admission, Financial Aid, and Communications on its three floors, and the mailroom in the basement. It has survived two fires (after the first one in 1889, a totally new structure was built), one major renovation that completely changed the exterior face of the house, several smaller renovations, and two votes by the Regents to tear it down. For decades it served as the official Vice-Chancellor's residence.

Several of the Fulford Hall staff who have worked on the main floor admit to seeing the "shadow man" all the time. If you are in the main room, you can hear him unless you turn music on. If you go into the back hallway, you can see him lingering in the far left doorway across from the stairs. Two staff members used to bring their big dogs to work with them at night, and neither dog would go willingly down that back hall. One would crawl and the other simply refused to go. One person was followed by footsteps across the front porch that kept going to the edge after she jumped off the end of the porch. Some staff members see or feel this person every day.

There is a student office near the kitchen in the back of the house. The students have seen the shadow man. One night when they were leaving the office, the computer suddenly started playing music.

In 2008 while undergoing renovation, Fulford Hall let go of a secret – a human femur was found in the wall. The best guess about how it ended up there is that for a period of time the house was used as an infirmary when the hospital was being rebuilt after a fire gutted that structure, and the residence also housed medical students for a time.

Fulford is not the only house in town where human bones have been discovered. When the University had a medical school, from 1892 to 1909, it was apparently common for students to use their anatomy cadavers in more places than the lab. Their methods for obtaining those cadavers also remain questionable. Apparently these and other "traditions" were common at all medical colleges at the time. The University possesses pictures of med students surrounded by cadavers, another common practice among medical students. Naturally, no one had heard of surgical masks, gloves, or other sanitary measures, either, as is evident by photos of their labs.

In 2013 I went back to Fulford Hall to ask staff if the shadow man was still there. I thought that perhaps finding the bone in the wall satisfied the apparition. Apparently, however, he is still there shuffling around in the back stairwell and following people across the front porch. Maybe he is curious about prospective students. Perhaps he likes the activity in the building, or maybe he wants to complete an unfinished task. Whatever the reason, it will take more than merely removing a femur from a wall to get rid of him.

It is rumored that the spirit is that of the beloved Spanish teacher Senor William Waters Lewis, and that he died from a fall down the Fulford stairs. An obituary for him makes that seem quite possible. His death was the result of a fall on his 89th birthday when leaving a Commencement reception. Receptions were held at the Vice Chancellor's house, which at that time was Fulford Hall! If so, he likely craves company. He was always entertaining students at his house. He reportedly haunts the Delt House as well.

Gailor Hall

One would think that Gailor Hall would have many stories attached to it, especially since an actual suicide took place in this hall when it was a dorm and cafeteria. This was where William Boone Massey shot himself after discovering that his best friend had committed suicide. People have hinted at stories from the "old days," especially in the basement, but no real stories have materialized from that time period.

There is, however, one story that took place after the renovation that converted Gailor into an academic building for English and foreign languages.

Downstairs in the space outside the auditorium are two tables where students often study. One afternoon James and John were down there studying. James was at the large table and John the smaller one. When James looked up, he saw a figure in a pea coat standing behind John. A few seconds later he disappeared into thin air! John didn't see a thing.

Guerry Hall

When you are over at Guerry
Those ghosts may make you quite wary
They're inside and out
Without any doubt
And the places they haunt often vary.

Guerry Hall was originally built in the 1950's as a performing arts hall. It now houses the music department but still has a stage used for all kinds of events. The art gallery is a two story, windowless room that connects Guerry Hall with Convocation Hall. The gallery opens four exhibits a year. Students staff the desk to keep statistics and enhance security.

Tamika worked in the art gallery in Guerry Hall, and one day she and Gary were locking up. They turned off the lights and shut the door so they could arm the security system. They set the alarm, and then went to open the door to leave. It wouldn't open. It felt as though there was someone holding the door closed on the other side. They tried for about ten minutes, but the door stubbornly refused to budge. Gary went to the phone to call the police to come break down the door or call a locksmith or do whatever it took to get them out of there. As soon as he finished dialing the number, Tamika tried the door again, and it opened with ease. They left the building quickly!

A Little More Guerry

Sherri spent a lot of time in Guerry since she was a music major and used the practice rooms there. Many times she would feel someone standing beside her or behind her, but when she looked nobody was there. A toilet flushed by itself in the bathroom when she was the only one in there.

Avery heard footsteps following her into the women's restroom as her friend waited for her in the outer room. Her friend did not notice a thing. Avery and Sherri are not the only ones who have experienced those sensations. Others have seen a figure in the auditorium watching them from a particular balcony as they worked backstage or in the rafters. Guerry is the building that held the old organ from All Saints Chapel for several years. The ghost who played the organ in All Saints followed the organ to Guerry and was occasionally heard playing it even though it was not in working condition by that time.

Outside Guerry

One night Sam was walking home. It was a foggy night, which is not that unusual for Sewanee. As he was walking, he saw something strange. It was a figure in a long white gown, like an old-fashioned nightgown. The figure, a woman, appeared to be only partially materialized. She was crossing the road at a cross walk on Georgia Avenue, coming from the direction of St. Luke's Chapel. She crossed the walk and went up to the basement windows on the east side of Guerry Hall. She paused to peer in the windows.

Sam couldn't believe what he was seeing. He called out a random name. "Sarah!" The specter looked up and turned towards him. As Sam stood, transfixed, yet terrified, the figure turned around and floated into the fog. Many others have seen this spirit both in that location and in front of Carnegie Hall inside the quadrangle.

Those who wish to put a name to a face believe that this is the spirit of Mrs. DuBose, wife of theology professor and chaplain William Porcher DuBose. There was a chaplain's house on the site of Guerry hall, but the DuBoses did not ever live there. They did live nearby, though. They lived in a rectory near where McClurg, the dining hall, is today, beside All Saints Chapel. Perhaps it is Mrs. DuBose, and perhaps it is someone who is not happy that the beautiful chaplain's house was taken down to build Guerry Hall.

Juhan Gym, The Old Swimming Pool, and Abbo's Alley

Before the Fowler Center was built in the 1990's, the athletic center was known as the Juhan Gym. The Fowler Center was built around and incorporated most of the old gym, just as the Juhan Gym was built around an even older Gym. This site also happens to be on the path of a stagecoach road and next door to the site of an old inn that predates the University. It is also close to a site of the activities that occurred during the founding events of the University, including an August 1858, picnic that involved the entire county plus many guests and prospective investors from other states, and also the 1860 Cornerstone ceremony. The stream that served as the main source of water for years is behind this gym. A cabin built by Lawson Rowe (or Lanson – both versions appear in county records) and later owned by Mr. Rutledge stood nearby.

One area of the Juhan Gym that was completely redone when the new fitness center was built was the old swimming pool area. It used to be off the east side of the gym that now houses a bouldering wall. As long as that swimming pool was used, all college students had to pass a swim test as part of graduation requirements. More than one student failed to graduate because of this. Just like the new pool, the old one was open to the public at various times.

Locker Room Ghost

Timothy was lifeguarding at the old gym pool in the summer of '91. He was bored to death during the 7:00 - 8:30 p.m. shift. Only three people came in - a mother with her two daughters, who were probably 9 to 12 years old with dark hair. They left at 8:15 and, being the good worker he was, he waited until 8:30 to shut things down. As he was on the tennis-court side of the pool turning out lights, he noticed a girl with blondish hair, possibly 4 to 6 yrs old wearing a white dress, going into the women's locker room. Totally dismissing any notion that he may have seen a ghost, he assumed that one of the girls that had come in earlier had forgotten something, even though they were older and had dark brown hair. Timothy waited for twenty minutes for this person to come out of the locker room before he went in to look for her. He found nothing. He told this story to local worker Carl Pless, who said that he had seen a similar looking blonde girl in a white "Easter type" dress and a white bow in her hair in Abbo's Alley gesturing towards the gym. She disappeared before his eyes.

After the new pool was built, Sewanee organized a popular community swim team. Dora was a member of the swim team when she saw a little girl in the pool who was obviously a ghost. After that she refused to return to the swim team.

Others have talked about a little girl wandering around in the same area. A woman has been in touch recently to relate that her grandmother stayed at the Rowe cabin and buried a doll there to keep soldiers from stealing it (Sewanee having been a crossing place for both Federal and Confederate soldiers) and that they are still looking for the doll. Perhaps the little ghost girl is looking for it, too.

Kappa Sigma Archives House

The Author's Story

The Kappa Sigma house was originally built in the 1920's. The downstairs room had two exterior doors on each side of the house. In later years a small addition and a covered porch were added. When the fraternity closed down in 1970, the fraternity's faculty advisor bought the house and renovated it as a residence.

The Kappa Sigma house is now part of the University Archives. An addition on the back of the house holds its archives, rare books, and permanent collection of art and artifacts. A generous donor, a Kappa Sigma himself, purchased the building from private owners and renovated it into the elegant space it is now. I was the University Archivist when all of this came about and I and others have witnessed some things that suggest that we are not the sole occupants of the archives any more.

The first incident that happened was during a time I was working in the downstairs front room. The whole downstairs of the house is one large formal room that holds rare books. This happened as we were first moving books into the bookcases in the room. I worked by myself much of the time. I was putting books in the cases when I heard a cat yowl - loudly and persistently. It sounded as if it was coming from inside the house or just out the front door. I didn't see how a cat could have gotten in, but I investigated anyway because it sounded distressed. I looked through the house but found nothing, so I stepped out the front door. As soon as I opened the front door the yowling stopped. I looked around outside but saw no evidence of a kitty anywhere. I finally went back inside to continue shelving. As soon as I picked up a book to shelve, the cries started again. Again I went out onto the front porch and again the cries stopped. I looked around the building and yard but found nothing. This happened at least three more times. Finally Professor Tam Carlson came in. He was helping oversee the remodeling process for the owner and dropped by often to see how things were going. I implored him to go see if a cat was stuck in the basement. Let's just say that Tam never found a cat on the premises, and neither did I, though I heard the yowling on other occasions as well.

Another time during this move-in period my daughter and I went upstairs to play pool on the brand new pool table. Everyone knows that all fraternity houses (and former fraternity houses) must have pool tables. A conference table covers the pool table most of the time. We wanted to try it out before the cover came. We each checked the pockets to pull out the pool balls. One was missing. I was a little annoyed that someone would take one before the house even officially opened. But we played our game anyway. As we were finishing up, Dr. Carlson came in to check around. We went downstairs to greet him and I told him about the missing ball. He went upstairs, checked the pockets, and they were all accounted for!

One day I was filling the bookcases along the north wall. The cases all have glass doors that lock. I had the bookcase key and the front door key on my keychain with my other keys. I finished filling one of the cases and tossed the keys onto a nearby table to go across the room to check on something. When I came back to retrieve the keys, the two Kappa Sigma keys had come loose from the chain and were perfectly aligned together on the table, as if pointing to something. I actually looked around the room and said, "OK, I know you are really here."

My office was near the front room for a couple of years, and I heard lots of thumping and shuffling noises during that time in the front room like someone moving around, and upstairs too.

Now there has been a huge addition built onto the back of the house. The addition contains a reception room, a research room, and a gallery all on the main floor. Student assistants sit at the reception desk to greet people and to keep track of those who are visiting. They complained over and over about a screaming noise coming from the gallery that dissipated if they walked into the room, and also noticed that the house part of the building seemed to be very busy with footsteps and shuffling around, even though no one was there. That is still happening.

I like to think that the previous owner, political science professor Dr. Gilbert Gilchrist, is approvingly perusing the books in the room. We can only hope that Mrs. Gilchrist is satisfied with the renovation. Her tombstone, which she wrote herself, contains the following:

> Her creative spirit is manifest in her interior
> architectural redesign of the Kappa Sigma house
> which she transformed into a home in 1970. It is
> there she spent her final years delighting in her
> plants porch and five grand children.

It took the workmen about two days to undo all the renovation features she added to the house!

Rebel's Rest

While the tenants at Rebel's Rest
Try to sleep, those ghosts are a pest.
They knock on your door
And they party galore
It's nighttime when they're at their best.

If just one house in the Sewanee community could be haunted, Rebel's Rest would have been the most likely suspect. The sprawling building felt old and creaky and full of secrets. How many guests have encountered a paranormal piece of the past in that celebrated home? Tragically, a fire caused irreparable damage to the old home in the summer of 2014. Its memory will be preserved in physical ways, and let us hope that the several resident spirits find peace, or another place to call home.

Built in 1866 on the ashes of the Civil War, this log cabin was one of the oldest houses on the Domain of the University. There are only three other houses in the wider area that allege to have structures older than Rebel's Rest as part of them, and two of them are haunted as well.

Rebel's Rest remained in the family of George Rainsford Fairbanks for a full hundred years until the family donated it to the University to use as a guesthouse in 1966. Major Fairbanks, the first owner, is one of the few men associated with the founding of the University who survived to see the college open in 1868. He remained a loyal employee until his death. He is the author of the University's first official history, *The History of the University of the South*, published in 1909. His book was not updated until 2008. He is known as the author of a number of histories of Florida as well. Fairbanks served as the University's first lease officer. He worked with the first engineers, especially Charles Barney, when the University was being designed in the 1850's. According to some people, he never really left his Sewanee home.

Rebel's Rest had a casual check-in procedure. Usually the keys to the guests' rooms were left in a basket on the hall table inside the front door, with a note attached to them. Safety was not an issue. Sometimes there would be only one guest for the night.

During 2009 two people were staying at Rebel's Rest. One woman was giving a lecture on campus and one was passing through town. They stayed next door to each other in rooms B and C on the second floor, but were not acquainted with each other.

The woman from room C was tired the next day. She reported that she had been awakened no fewer than eight times by someone knocking on her door. Each time she answered the door, and each time no one was there. Once she wandered down to the kitchen and saw a woman with blonde hair in a long white gown floating around. Room C was a room on the second floor on the north side of the house that the custodians would not go into alone to clean because they had witnessed too many creepy things happening.

The woman in the next room, who by the way had dark hair, did not hear any knocking, but reported being awakened by loud snoring. When she got to Rebel's Rest late at night, it was unbearably hot inside. She found the thermostat turned up to 87 degrees. She turned it down to 75, but had to keep her window open that night in February.

The manager reported that the most common complaint from guests is that other "guests" were partying late into the night in the rooms downstairs. Some have even witnessed figures in nineteenth century clothing dancing and mingling. Others have complained that they heard children laughing and playing on the stairs and in the upstairs hallways all night. Stan was staying there and had been working on his computer. He closed his computer up and went to bed. As soon as he got into bed, he heard women laughing in the main room as if a party were going on.

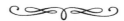

A number of years ago the guest rooms manager lived in one of the rooms on the first floor. She had many encounters with George Fairbanks. She knows this because the figure she always saw looked exactly like the portrait of Fairbanks that hung over the fireplace in the main room. (Fortunately, the portrait had been removed before the fire so it is still safe.)

One night her son came to spend the night with her. He was old enough to have been living on his own. He started out the night on the couch in the parlor, but soon came tearing into his mother's apartment. He had awakened to see George Fairbanks standing over him. He slept in his mom's room for the rest of the night.

One evening the manager was getting ready to go out. While she was in the bathroom she heard a tremendous crash. The poster over her bed that had been tacked to the wall had fallen, but no tacks had been moved at all, and no tears were in the poster. She saw the figure of George Fairbanks on many occasions in the outer rooms, but he did not come into her room. He seemed to be merely curious about how his house was being treated.

Sewanee Union Theater

The Sewanee Union Theater, or SUT as it is affectionately called, has been around for ages, attached to the back of Thompson Hall, which once served as a student union, snack bar, and student post office. It is a separate building from the Office of University Relations that now inhabits Thompson Hall, but a wide staircase used to lead right down the middle of the main floor to the basement where the movie theater is still located. The outer walls are made of pick-up stone, giving the place a cave like feel, and the old balcony gallery seating is still there, though not used. The films are equally outdated, usually already available on DVD or through streaming video, but it doesn't matter. The prices are comparable, and experimental films are still shown for free once a week.

In the past with older equipment the projectionist might have a little trouble transitioning between film reels, causing a short interruption somewhere in the middle of the movie. A man named George was projectionist for many years, and theatergoers used to assume he had fallen asleep when there was a big gap of time with a blank screen between reels. So people would call affectionately up to him: "GEOOOOOOORRRRRRGE." Actually, it was probably usually a malfunction of the ancient machinery (the original projector is still on display there), and he was quite good-natured to be a good sport about the student heckling (which was always good-natured, too). I think a few projectionists who came after George's time were called "George" too.

Being the last person out of the theater can be a spooky thing, especially if you have to go upstairs to the projection room where everything is musty and dark and shadowy.

Brianna, a high school student, worked at the theatre the one brief year the theater was contracted to an outside company. Each night after the movie was over she would go upstairs to shut off the projector and fax that night's paperwork to the managers. Because it was pretty creepy, she often had a friend stay after to go upstairs with her. One night there was no one available to go with her, so she went by myself. The door to the projector room didn't fit on the hinges exactly. When she passed through it, someone else passed through going the opposite direction. He was tall and was wearing old clothes and some type of brimmed hat. Brianna turned around immediately but he disappeared through the door. She never worked another night there by herself and quit two weeks later.

Could that have been George, by any chance?

Snowden Hall

Snowden Hall, built in 1962, is named in honor of J. Bayard Snowden of Memphis, Tennessee. The front, original part of the building has rooms paneled with native Tennessee wood. The addition was added in 2010 and features a large-scale solar installation and local stone and wood in its structure. It houses the departments of Geology, Forestry, and Natural Resources. Students who major in these fields are known to spend many hours in the building studying. It is no wonder they see the paranormal activity that occurs there after-hours.

Autumn has had several encounters with the Snowden ghost. She spent many, many nights in there until three and four in the morning, and heard footsteps upstairs several times. She would go to look for whoever was up there, but the building would be empty. As soon as she would get settled into the study room downstairs, she would hear the footsteps again. One night she thought she saw someone walking upstairs one night, just out of the corner of her eye, but when she turned to look, there was, of course, no one there. Autumn knows another girl who has seen the ghost. She is one of the few people who believed Autumn when she said she saw someone and heard footsteps.

Tennessee Williams Center

If Tennessee Williams knew
What the ghosts in the building there do
He'd be very pleased
To know that they teased
And he'd want to be part of it too.

In this performing arts studio in Sewanee you are able to hear noises from clapping to screaming in the former pool area. It is said that when the building was first constructed as a gym for Sewanee Military Academy students, a young boy drowned in the pool and no one witnessed it. He will clap for you from time to time or he will taunt you with a scream. There is not a news story to verify that anyone ever drowned in the pool. It is rumored that the pool is actually still in the building. It just has a floor over it. Before the gym was built there was a very nice house there. The gym was converted to a performing arts center using part of a bequest from Tennessee Williams, who surprised the University by leaving them the rights to his plays.

Two custodians, Rhonda and Michelle, were cleaning the Tennessee Williams building one morning and were the only ones there. It was about 6:30 in the morning. They were in the basement where the costume department is and they had just finished cleaning the women's bathroom. Michelle had already left the room. Rhonda was leaving the bathroom when suddenly all of the faucets came on at once. Startled, she steeled herself and braved the room long enough to turn them off. She high-tailed it to the door to get out of there as quickly as possible but again the faucets came on in concert. Once again she turned them off. At that point she looked around the room and told the spirits to stop; that she did not want to clean up water again. They did not come back on that day. That happened randomly several times, by the way.

Once again on a different morning, the two were working together at the Tennessee Williams building. They were just finishing up the building for the day when Michelle said to Rhonda, "I just saw someone in the sewing room windows." Rhonda looked but didn't see anything at first. She resumed vacuuming the foyer but stopped because she heard someone come up behind her. She turned around to look and saw a man in the sewing room window watching her.

Several students have mentioned that they have encountered spooks or spooky incidents in the building, including the water turning on and off by itself.

It is a bit freaky to be in that building alone! Tennessee Williams would probably like that.

Thompson Hall

One would expect Thompson Hall to be haunted, and not because its original beautiful, elegant, three story structure was torched in 1950 and the renovated building was so plain in comparison. It is not because students and faculty (perhaps now deceased ones) bemoan the fact that the building is no longer the center of activity on campus as it was when it was the Student Union, sandwich shop, and post office, or because of all the plays and dances and other social activities that drew the entire campus to play there. It is not even because it went through a number of years of identity crisis when the University couldn't decide how best to utilize it and thus it became a center for storage, or rather a junk mecca, with a couple of pianos thrown in to see if it would make a good music practice building. Thompson Hall has better reasons to have spirits wandering around at night (or during the day). Thompson was built as "Chemical and Philosophical Hall" in the 1880's, but became more specifically the Medical Department from 1892-1909. What that means is that Thompson Hall saw its share of anatomy classes and cadavers. Well, from where did those cadavers come? Photos of students proudly surrounded by deceased anatomy buddies reveal the less than ideal cleanliness of the place, the lack of gloves and masks and sterile environments. But mostly, they show a lack of respect for the dead bodies. Who knows whether they came from legitimate sources or whether they left that place with the same bones and bodies they came with, or where or if they were ever properly buried or cremated.

Nowadays, Thompson is the mecca for raising money for the University. Offices and cubicles are carved into all kinds of little pockets and corners. Carla has one such office tucked into a back corner of the first floor, across the hall from a room that coincidentally opens onto the second floor of the theater where the haunted projection room is.

One night Carla was working late. When she first heard activity across the hall, she assumed that another staff member was still there working in the file room. Maybe it was the custodian. Yes, that's who it was. Jacob. She was getting ready to leave around 8 p.m. when she heard a door creak open and shut. Then she heard footsteps. "Bye Jacob,"she called out. The footsteps headed up the hallway. Carla stepped to her doorway to say goodbye again. To her astonishment, nobody was there.

"Now was he really walking fast enough to turn into main room before I got to the door?" Carla was thinking. "Maybe it was Cindy." Cindy worked in the office up the hall. "Jacob?" She called, walking down the hallway now. "Cindy?" Cindy's locked office door stared at her like a disapproving schoolmarm.

Footsteps. They were in the main room now.

"Jacob! That you?" Carla rounded the corner to the main room.

Silence.

She stopped. She looked around. Clearly nobody was in the room. It took about ten seconds - ten incredibly long seconds. Her curiosity suddenly exploded into fear. Someone was there, yet she couldn't see him. Carla sprinted back to her office, her heart in her throat. A thousand thoughts stormed through her head. Was it a staff member playing a joke — a bad one? A prowler? A meth-crazed serial killer? She listened only for the sound of more footsteps, and she watched the front door. Five minutes passed. Ten. The footsteps had merely vanished, like the person. No one had left the room. She would have heard the door opening because it squeaked. Had she imagined it?

Then she knew. It was the only thing that could explain the many times both she and others had heard footsteps and rummaging in the back room, at odd times of the day and night. Now Carla is on the lookout for the ghost of Thompson Union.

Van Ness

That ghost at Van Ness Hall
He has an abundance of gall
He likes to possess
And cause great duress
To visitors one and all.

Jabez Hayes built the first house on the site of the Van Ness building in 1871. Mr. Hayes also ran a sawmill and built quite a few houses in the area during the early years. The first person to live in the house was Professor Dabney, who was also the first professor to die at Sewanee, at age 42, and the first ghost reported in Sewanee. He did not die in this house. The Juny family inhabited the house the longest. They boarded many students there.

The US Forest Service built the building called Van Ness in the 1960's as a silviculture lab. When they closed down, it became an annex of the Music department, including the piano practice rooms. This ghost story took place during that time period. The building has now been demolished and the Ayres dorm is being built in its place. Will the evil ghost that haunted Van Ness stick around to plague students?

The story goes like this: Frederick, a music major, was practicing piano in Van Ness Hall. There was one practice room with a baby grand piano while all the rest had uprights. He was playing that baby grand and hanging out with his girlfriend when they both saw a shadow pass by the window accompanied by a low, animal-like growl (not a growl, not a bark, not a woof...more like a growlf). They thought it was weird, but resumed their conversation and piano playing. The shadow passed the window again with another growlf, this time louder.

Frederick got very still and started improvising a piece in an ominous minor key, something neither he nor his girlfriend had ever heard before. His girlfriend asked him why he was playing this odd piece, and Frederick didn't respond. He seemed in a trance-like state, and he began to play louder and faster and wilder. His girlfriend tried to rouse him from his trance and wasn't able to. He just became more agitated and manic. Finally, she pulled him away from the piano, and he started screaming and wouldn't stop. She led him to his car and, since it was late at night, she did the only thing she could think of and drove him to the Chapel. He was screaming and flailing the whole time, and it was all she could do to pull him out of his car and up the Chapel steps.

She opened the door of the Chapel, and he suddenly stopped screaming. He seemed dazed and disoriented, and he asked her what happened and why they were at the door of the Chapel. He had no recollection of what happened, the piece he was playing, or anything after the second time they saw the shadow go past the window.

Frederick refused ever to practice or even step foot in the baby grand room again, and who can blame him!

Another very talented piano player was practicing in the same room in Van Ness late one night, and he also started improvising and found himself playing a very creepy song and felt as if he had no control over it.

Author's Note

The possession story was the first story I received that seemed really terrifying. I used to practice in that building myself, and remember that only one room actually had a baby grand in it.

After hearing this story recounted in 2008, I went to the building to reacquaint myself with that room, and found that all the rooms had baby grands!

I used to play in the orchestra at Sewanee, and was talking one night with a new member. She and her family had moved to Sewanee earlier that year, and she was telling me about a ghost in her rental home in the Woodlands housing area. Then she said, "Have you ever heard anything about Van Ness?" Having just received the "possession" story, I said, "Have YOU heard anything?" She told me she took her child to practice there, but that she would not let him practice in "the room with the baby grand" because there was a bad aura in that room. I have since asked several music majors what they think, and they all agree that the building is creepy.

One student wrote to me and said, "I'm so glad to hear other people are as creeped out by Van Ness as I am. I used to practice there late at night and would always pick up my stuff and run as fast as I could to my car when I finished."

When my children were little they took violin lessons in Van Ness Hall. My daughter was terrified of the parking lot. There was a tree that pelted acorns on her as if they were attacking her. The only odd thing I ever encountered was a neighbor's goat that came over and walked on the cars!

Walsh-Ellett

The spook at Walsh likes to turn
The lights on and off, you will learn
He walks down the hall
Not stopping to call
And leaves you with lots of concern.

Walsh Hall was built as one of the first stone academic buildings. The Ellett name became associated with the building during its first renovation. Surrounded by cloisters, it overlooks the main campus quadrangle. The second floor rooms open out onto an outdoor walkway. During class changes this can be a busy social area of campus. The building houses the History and Economics departments. Administrative offices cover the first floor.

Jacob studied in the classrooms in Walsh-Ellett during the late 1980's and remembers hearing phantom footsteps and doors slamming. No one was ever there when he checked out the noises.

Robert was studying on the third floor of Walsh-Ellett one night and heard footsteps in the hallway. He thought it was a friend coming to visit. He waited as the footsteps got closer and closer. He watched as the footsteps passed by the door. No legs or body accompanied the footsteps. They continued and went down the stairwell. Robert grabbed his things and ran out. He decided to study at home for the rest of the night.

For others the lights in the classrooms would turn on and off as they pleased. Now the lights are on motion switches. Many students who have tried to study in Walsh have told the same stories.

There is a set of spiral staircases at the front end of the building, and you are supposed to go up the "out" staircase and down the "in" one. If you go the other way the ghost of a soldier might be at the exit to let you know you went the wrong way. It's not just a sign to others to let them know you are a freshman who doesn't know any better yet.

Woods Lab

Woods Lab, named for J. Albert Woods, opened in 1965 and supplied a much needed new science and math hall. Later the top floor was finished out for psychology and anthropology classrooms. It is also equipped with computer classrooms. An addition onto Woods Lab called Spencer Hall provides additional classroom, laboratory, office, and lounge space. It is not unusual for students to study in these buildings late into the night.

Prana was studying late one night on the third floor of Woods. It was the only place she could get an internet signal. Around 3 or 3:30 a.m. she heard a noise from the closet in the back of the classroom. She went back to investigate but found only empty animal cages in the closet. A few minutes later the window, which was already open, began swinging back and forth. This lasted for about fifteen minutes, then stopped. There was no wind to explain the flapping. Prana decided she had studied enough for that night!

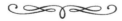

Karen was the Department of Anthropology's student assistant, and she used to work on the third floor late at night a lot, usually at the copier. She would at times hear footsteps behind her, but no one would ever be there when she turned around to check. It always sent shivers down her back, but she usually braved the noises. One night she heard them a lot, and then suddenly, the copier turned off. The power wasn't out. There were still lights, but she never could get the copier to come back on that night.

Author's Note

I received one really detailed, well-written story about a ghostly encounter a student and her boyfriend had in Woods Lab. It involved, among many other details I cannot remember, keys locked in a room, doors systematically slamming one by one on the second floor and then the third floor, and a sighting, but that story, saved with several others on several of my computers and back-up hard drives, along with the name of its author, has been wiped clean. I even had a printed copy of it, but apparently it is destined NOT to be in this book!

Dormitories and Student Centers

Ayres Multicultural Center

The Ayres Multicultural Center began life as a gathering place for students who chose not to join a fraternity. By the mid-seventies it housed the Assistant Chaplain and served as a student performance center/coffee house called the Outside Inn. It was completely student run, a place where students could put on plays, sing, or otherwise entertain on campus. Then, for a long time in the 1980's, it remained empty. Now, as the Ayres Multicultural Center, it is used for a multitude of social and educational events.

During the time that the center was uninhabited two friends, Sheila and James, used to sneak into the Outside Inn to spend the night. They would borrow firewood from the Fiji house, a nearby fraternity house, make fires in the nice stone fireplace, and sleep on the floor. One night when they spent the night there, Sheila was awakened by the sound of someone rustling through the fallen leaves outside, approaching the building. "James, wake up, wake up!" she whispered, but of course to no avail.

The doors lining the performance space were glass French doors that also served as big windows. You could enter and leave through these doors to the outdoors. Sheila saw a man standing at one of them, looking down at them on the floor. He was wearing what could be described as 19th century clothes, with an umbrella or a cane in his hand. While she was looking, the man vanished before her eyes. He was simply gone. He left no footsteps or other indication that he could have been there. Chills ran through

Sheila's spine. After that she and James slept in the loft, and pulled the ladder up behind them.

Bairnwick Women's Center

The women at Bairnwick Hall
Think Margaret often does call.
She wafts up the stairs
Scaring girls into prayers
And sometimes comes right through the wall.

The Women's Center on campus was originally a private residence, "Bairnwick," built for the Myers family. The Rev. George Boggan Myers taught at the School of Theology from the twenties through the fifties. Mrs. Margaret Myers, his wife, taught a private school in their home for twenty years. The house saw much activity, as the Myers raised eight children, ran the school there, and kept guests constantly. The house had an extra lease with its own barn for chickens and cows, a tennis court, and other playground equipment. The house always had a dog or two, the most famous of whom was Hrothgar, the English bulldog. The ghost of the house is reportedly Mrs. Myers, who died in the master bedroom on the third floor in 1970.

After the house was deeded to the University, it served briefly as the University's first language house (the French house), and then as the School of Theology's extension center before taking on its current role as the Women's Center. It has never ceased to have lots of activity, apparently some of it paranormal.

Kelly saw a little boy in older clothing looking out the third floor window. Then he suddenly disappeared. Natalie was in the library when she suddenly heard music as if coming from a jukebox.

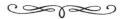

In 2009, Caroline, a student resident of the house, saw a woman disappearing into her room on the third floor. Curious, though not afraid, Caroline inquired at the University Archives for a photograph of Mrs. Myers. The Archives found one of her driving her "dual colored contraption," a golf cart, in 1966. She and her husband had always gotten around on a motorcycle with a sidecar, but after he died she invested in the golf cart, a new phenomenon on campus. It sped up to seven miles an hour. A friend of hers made a lovely fringe to go around the top.

There Mrs. Myers was in the picture, sitting up as straight as an arrow in her coat and hat, ready to take on the town. She was the perfect likeness of the spirit patrolling Bairnwick's third floor.

Kate lived for a year in Bairnwick on the third floor. To her it always felt pretty spooky. One event was particularly interesting. When she came back from spring break, she rearranged the furniture in her room. That night, as she was sitting on her bed doing some reading for class, she looked over to her dresser and all three of the open drawers slammed closed at once! Then she felt as if dry ice had been welded into her sternum. There must have been some force because the weight of the drawers and the tilt of the room kept them open most of the time. Spooky. She ran into her neighbor's room. Her neighbor had had experiences with ghosts when she lived in another dorm on campus, and she talked to the ghost for Kate. The next day Kate put her room back the way it had been and that was the end of Spookfest '07.

One evening Celia was sitting in the common room on the second floor doing schoolwork. She heard someone walk up the stairs to the second floor and naturally assumed it was one of the residents. Because of where she was sitting, Celia could see the reflection of the hallway in the far window of the common room. In the reflection she saw a figure. She assumed it was her roommate walking down the hallway towards their room. Celia called her name but got no response, so she quickly got up and left the common room to talk to her only to realize that not only was she not there but also that the house was entirely empty.

There were also plenty of times when Celia was studying in a secluded nook on the third floor when she was suddenly overwhelmed by a strange smell. It didn't smell like anything familiar, and it wasn't a particularly good or bad smell. The only description she had of the smell is that it was somewhat old and musty. It could, of course, just have been the old house, but she found it peculiar that it didn't continuously smell that way. When she did smell it, however, it was wafting about and centralized in that corner of the house. It generally lasted for several hours.

After Celia posted her stories Mary, a Women's Center alum of '04, dropped by. Celia asked her about her experiences in this house. She confirmed the musty smell in the corner of the third floor. She also remembered smelling oranges in the hallway of the third floor, which was confirmed by yet another Bairnwick resident. Mary also said that room 31 on the third floor, which has a door opening directly to the porch, was visited by the possible ghost of Mrs. Myers. Apparently the external door would occasionally open – even if locked – right after one a.m., which was supposedly the time Mrs. Myers did room checks when she kept women visiting campus, to make sure the women were home and in bed. Mrs. Myers, according to her son, slept only five hours a night.

Most excitingly, Mary related her first-hand account of seeing Mrs. Myers downstairs in the Women's Center, walking from the large room where Women's Center sponsored luncheons are held (a room added by the University after her death as a venue for large events) to the adjacent green room.

Others have reported seeing Mrs. Myers as well. At least one student moved from the house because of the hauntings. Many women have heard footsteps on the stairs, usually footsteps late at night, sometimes accompanied by a sound like ice clinking in a glass. It's Mrs. Myers retiring upstairs with her favorite nightcap, brandy on the rocks.

Benedict Hall

At 11 p.m. one night during the Young Writers' conference, Candace heard screaming coming from one of the rooms above the entrance. Bella came tearing downstairs. She had just gone into her bathroom and seen a girl standing there hovering four inches above the ground. Everyone stayed up late that night!

Cannon Hall

Cannon Hall has recently taken its place at the top of the list of Sewanee's swank residence halls, just as it was when it opened in the 1920's as an award-winning example of architecture. The year 2012 marks the year of Cannon's renovation and expansion. For at least fifty years, however, Cannon Hall had a secure spot on the "dingier dorm" list.

It was one of those dorms that defied the assumption that students only want to live in upscale dormitories. Cannon Hall had no air conditioning, communal bathrooms, and some very small rooms, but, like some of the old dingier spaces of the past (there were the dilapidated Woodlands or Selden barracks with their holes in walls and floors, outdated bathrooms, and certain appeal to rats and other wildlife, or lower Gailor with its clanky pipes running across the ceiling, grease pit smell, and claustrophobic feel), students who lived in Cannon often stayed there more than one year. In these dorms there often were not head residents, and certain rules could be overlooked in exchange for the shabby surroundings.

Cannon Hall is located halfway down South Carolina Avenue, on the site of the former Sedley Ware house, which burned around 1923. In that spectacular fire, one of many in the older times at Sewanee, the Wares escaped with barely the clothes on their backs, and Dr. Ware lost nineteen years' worth of research notes.

Cannon Hall, named for former chaplain John Brown Cannon, was originally planned to be built beside its sister dorm, Johnson Hall, which was designed by the same architect, but after the Ware house burned, that site became the preferred location for the new dorm.

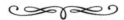

Derek lived in Cannon Hall during the mid-1980's. Derek, who is now a doctor, became quite disturbed by ghostly visits in his room. Spirits had a habit of swirling about the room, usually after he went to bed.

When Heather was a sophomore at Sewanee in the fall of 1989, she had an encounter with a ghost in a small restroom in Cannon. The restroom was on an upper floor on the end of the building. It was dark outside. The light bulb in the room was burned out, but there was a window, and so between streetlights and the moon, she could see well enough.

While Heather was washing her hands she looked into the mirror and saw a reflection that was not her own. It was a woman, but she had her brown hair up in a chignon and had on a high-necked dress with lace around the collar of the dress. It appeared to be a fashion from the turn of the century (from the 19th to the 20th, that is, not the present century).

Heather had shoulder-length blonde hair at the time and it was down that night. She was wearing a vivid blue and green print wrap dress with a plunging neckline. She was definitely not seeing her own reflection. The apparition in the mirror was not frightening or threatening; she was simply there. It did, however, make enough of an impression to burn the details into Heather's memory. Though she was not afraid at the time, she was not keen to go into that bathroom again.

Since the renovation the spirit has let it be known to others that she is still around.

Who was the ghost? Was she Mrs. Ware or one of the many ladies who stayed with them? Perhaps one day she will be seen again.

Is she the same supernatural presence that several students have reported feeling upstairs in Cannon?

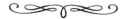

Cannon is now connected to a new dormitory, Smith Hall. In order to build Smith Hall the University had to take down a small historic cottage on the site. A student who had recently lived in that cottage reported that there was often loud banging on the roof of the cottage. The little house held another secret under its floor that was revealed when the floor was taken apart: a nest of copperheads!

Cleveland Hall

The Cleveland ghost stays busy
Keeping girls there in a tizzy
A blessing was made
But the spook still paid
Enough visits to make them all dizzy.

Stories about this dorm brought forward the question of exorcisms. Word was that the University Chaplain provided exorcisms for rooms in Cleveland, Tuckaway, and Hoffman at various times. The official word from the former Assistant Chaplain is that only a Bishop can perform an exorcism (at least in the Episcopal Church), and that all those dorms received blessings but not exorcisms. All of the dorms are still plagued by spirits, too.

Cleveland is a three story stone building on University Avenue across the street from the University's Book and Supply Store. The first two floors contain suites with two double rooms divided by a central study area. The third floor, in the eaves, consists of single and double rooms. Bathrooms are located at each end of each hall. Cleveland Hall replaced Barton Hall, a set of WWII barracks plopped onto that site. The Barton barracks replaced Barton Hall, a house built by a professor in 1873 and later used as a boarding house for many years. The Barton barracks burned, but the front façade did not fall, so for a while it was a little disconcerting to walk past it and discover nothing behind.

There are ghost stories related to all three floors of Cleveland Hall, this dorm that sits so conveniently close to classrooms and the dining hall. Though Cleveland was built before women were first admitted to Sewanee, it became a women's dorm shortly afterwards, and has only recently became co-ed.

Close Your Door!

Emily lived in Cleveland her freshman year and remembers having the front door to her suite close on its own every now and then. She and her suitemates grew accustomed to the situation but it was still strange every time it happened. It wasn't until some years later that someone told her that a student had been raped in Cleveland by a stranger off the streets. As the story she heard goes, the woman was screaming as the assault was occurring, but since it was a weekend night, all the other girls in the dorm just thought she was drunk. They closed their doors to her screams, so she now wanders the halls and closes people's doors. The woman allegedly committed suicide in her dorm room at the end of the school year. No one ever heard about it because nearly everyone had already left school for summer vacation.

Amy witnessed ghostly experiences repeatedly in Cleveland 305. Many nights in a row during her senior year she would wake up in the middle of the night and then shortly feel the sensation that someone had just sat down on the end of her bed by her feet. No one was ever visible, but she could feel someone sit down there. Strangely, she was never scared at the time. She would go back to sleep and then get really freaked out when she remembered it in the morning. Reportedly lots of Cleveland residents that year had strange stories like this.

Terrill lived in Cleveland 305 during her senior year. For some reason her heat stayed on all year, even though she turned it off constantly. One night she woke up and something was pushing her down into her bed. She slept with the lights on for two weeks after that.

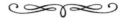

Melissa lived on the first floor of Cleveland. She woke one night to find a little boy in her room. When she sleepily asked him what he was doing there, he backed up without a sound and disappeared into the wall.

Delilah had a room on the second floor. She had to yell at the ghost to stop slamming the doors. There were no real people around to be doing the slamming. Another time she was writing a paper late at night. She went to use the restroom down the hall at around 2:30 a.m. As she was in the stall, she heard someone open the door next to her and go quietly into the stall. She could see the shadow on the ground. When Delilah came out of her stall, no one was there. She had the feeling it was a quiet, shy teenaged girl.

Thanksgiving Ghost

When Elizabeth lived in Cleveland her freshman year, she and her friend were two of only four girls left in the dorm over Thanksgiving and the only two on the second floor. One afternoon, while Elizabeth was down the hall from her room talking to her friend, her door suddenly slammed shut and locked her out. No one else was around. Once they found someone to let Elizabeth in, they examined the room and found not a single way that a draft of air could have blown it shut. All the windows were closed in her dorm room and everyone else's doors were closed and locked. Creepy? They figured that since the "demon suffocator" was exorcised from the first floor years before, the ghost had simply moved one floor up!

Demon Suffocator

Author's Note: What is all this about a murderous ghost on Cleveland's first floor? I got this tale directly from the Head Resident, who allowed me and a small band of elementary school followers to go into the infamous suite where the ghost preyed on students. It was a suite where two of my friends had once lived, suite 102-103!

In the group of girls assigned to that suite that year, Rebecca and Shelby were friends who decided to room together, and Rivers, their suitemate, was a student whose roommate did not come back to school so she ended up with a single for the semester. That almost never happens, so people considered her lucky. Rivers was a little bit spacey, and had some kooky ideas, but she was fine as a suitemate.

The first night the girls went to bed, Rivers was not in her room five minutes before she ran back into the study and announced to her suitemates that someone had tried to get into bed with her, and then tried to hold her down and smother her! She was quite upset, so the other girls calmed her down. When she finally got to bed she had horrible dreams and woke up out of breath. Within a few days Rivers had found another place to stay. That side of the suite stayed empty for the rest of the semester. The suitemates chalked the whole thing up to her being kind of strange to begin with. They did not have any trouble for the rest of the semester.

For the second semester, a friend of the suitemates, Donna, decided to move in with them. She, unlike the first girl, was very grounded and level-headed. The first night they retired kind of late. Sleep, however, was not in the stars for them. Within five minutes Donna was knocking frantically on her friends' door. Someone, she said, had tried to suffocate her in her own bed! They had the room blessed, but she still slept in the study room all semester.

A year later Emma was locked into suite 102-103 one day. Then, when she finally got out of the room she went to the bathroom across the hall, and one of the faucets turned itself on. She did not stick around long enough to see if it turned itself off again. Something still haunts Cleveland dorm.

Cleveland dorm was one of the summer music school dorms for many years. One music student, Chloe, looked up one night to find a pale young woman dressed in 19th Century clothing standing at the foot of her bed smiling at her. The next morning, her roommates found their violin cases open and their music strewn across the floor. The next night, the same thing happened to a girl who lived across the hall.

Another night, Chloe was lying in her bed in trying to fall asleep. All of a sudden, she felt a warmth in her right ear. She could feel that someone was whispering in her ear, but she could not make out anything that was being said. Then, it felt like someone had gotten in the bed with her and then, a force pushed her head up against the wall. She jumped out of bed and ran out into the hall, terrified, but everyone was asleep so she gradually got the courage to go back into her room. She finally convinced herself that it was a dream. The next morning she awoke with a huge goose egg and a bruise on her forehead.

Who knows how many others have encountered the ghosts of Cleveland dorm!

Courts

Courts is one of three dorms in Sewanee built around a central courtyard. Each suite is designed with two bedrooms and two study rooms joined by a communal bathroom. This dorm is located near the University cemetery.

Nicole's room was on the first floor next to one of the entries to the courtyard. One night Nicole woke in the night to see a tall man standing over her roommate. She thought it was a student who was about to assault her roommate. Terrified, she tried to think how to get to her phone to call the police.

She moved her hand slightly and suddenly the figure had jumped, or flown, across the room and was on top of her. It wasn't a body; it was a spirit figure. The spirit pushed her down into her bed, making her feel winded and unable to catch a breath. There seemed to be nothing she could do. She was going to die — she knew it. After the longest minute of her life, the figure suddenly vanished. Nicole spent a sleepless night considering what had happened. This happened to her again a couple of weeks later. Nicole moved to a different dorm the next year.

Barbara lived on the second floor of Courts facing the lake. One day she was in her room when she saw a man enter the adjoining suite all dressed up in a big 1920's fur coat. When she went in to investigate the man vanished. Her suitemates' alarm clocks and stereos were turned off quite a few times when they knew they were set properly, too. Were all these occurrences the doing of the same spirit?

Delta Kappa Epsilon House

Two normally obedient dogs belonging to DEKE members refused to go into a certain area around the house. One even tucked his tail, afraid to move into the area.

When Donna came out of the downstairs restroom one evening, she heard the hangers in the nearby closet scraping against the door. Since no one else heard it, she figured she was just hearing things, until Stewart came over, looked into the closet and asked who shifted his hangers.

Delta Tau Delta House

The Delta Tau Delta fraternity, one of the five oldest on campus, meets in a Tudor style house on University Avenue across the street from where the original cornerstone to the University was laid in 1860. That house is home to more than just fraternity members. Quite a few students would agree that paranormal activity occurs at the Delt house.

Adam has heard and seen the doors in the house close by themselves. He has heard footsteps on the stairs only to find no one there when he looked. He has also heard footsteps behind him while coming up the stairs and turned to see who had come up behind him and there would be no one. The noises on the stairs and the closing doors happen both day and night.

One encounter was quite vivid and could not be explained by drafts, old house noises, and the other things that could typically be the reason behind some of the "ghost" encounters. Adam had gone to the Delt House on a Wednesday night in February with his roommate and a friend to watch *South Park*. The fraternity was shut down that semester for some reason, but the house still had cable television, so they would go over every week and quietly go up to the TV room to watch a few shows. They were not drinking, as they always thought it would be enough trouble to get caught in the house, let alone to have alcohol there. It was winter and cold and windy, and the house was pretty drafty, so they were used to strange noises.

As they were leaving, and rounding the bottom of the stairs, they heard a window opening loudly, as if someone had thrown it open as hard as they could. They froze immediately. All the lights were off, since they were trying not to make it apparent that people were in the house. Adam peeked around the corner to the room with the pool table and the back door out to the deck through which they had entered. He half expected to see one of the police officers looking through a window at him.

The first strange thing he saw was that the window was still open. This window was over the "pit" (the stairs to the basement, where fraternity members tended to throw bottles to watch them break, dump trash, and more, a bad idea that the administration never liked). That window had been broken and replaced so many times (Adam had personally taken out the frame and replaced the glass twice), that all the counterweights that held the windows open had been disconnected or lost. The only way that window could stay up was to physically hold it or prop it with something. So it was a little freaky to see it just open with the cold wind coming through it. It was freezing in there too (more so than usual, which is saying a lot since the house was not heated).

As soon as this all raced through Adam's mind and he let out a stream of what was probably very colorful language, the window slammed shut. Logic catching up, he ran to the door, opened it, and turned on the light over the deck. No one was there. It was easy to tell that no one had been there since the deck was covered with fresh snow and there were no footprints under the window (or anywhere else on the deck). Adam and his friend looked at each other and then left quickly!

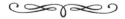

Andy, an alum and former fraternity member, related that he and all the other guys in the fraternity often heard shuffling around or steps shuffling behind them. Several women have declared that there is an apparition that shows itself only on the second floor, and only to women.

One explanation is the unsubstantiated story that the ghost is that of a guy who tried to hang himself from the fire escape. Some members of the fraternity insist that the ghost is the spirit of William Waters Lewis, a beloved Spanish professor who was very sociable, always having students to his house for tea. He was the DTD advisor while he was still alive. Others believe that Lewis inhabits Fulford Hall. There is no reason why Lewis could not be seen in both places. No one knows who it is for sure, but there is definitely a presence in that house.

Elliott Hall

The first lease at what used to be called "the forks," the intersection between University Avenue and Tennessee Avenue, belonged to the Phelan family. Judge Phelan from Alabama was reportedly a spy during the Civil War. His Alabama house was burned so he moved to the Mountain with his family (which apparently included several beautiful daughters). This family was related to Phelan Beale of Memphis and Beale Street fame.

After the judge's death the ladies opened a boarding house there. Then the University bought it, having in mind a Sewanee Hotel, for which they even sold stock. When that venture failed, the very large wooden structure was used by the students of the Sewanee Grammar School (later the Sewanee Military Academy) as a dormitory to "separate them from the bad influence of college students." When the grammar school moved to the newly built Quintard Hall in 1900, the house again served visitors.

The original house burned in the 1920's and Elliott Hall was built soon thereafter. Elliott became "The Sewanee Inn" when the current structure was built. A "new" Sewanee Inn was built in the

1960's. This building has since been razed to make way for an even newer Sewanee Inn.

There is only one small story currently associated with Elliott Hall. This is surprising since Elliott is one of only two dorms on campus that is known to have had a student suicide. (The other is Gailor, which is no longer a dorm.) A student killed himself in Elliott in the 1930's by taking strychnine. Mrs. Maude Kirby-Smith wrote about it in letters to her children. Her husband was the attending physician. This information did not make it into the newspapers.

Jeff was using the bathroom at around three in the morning in mid-October, 2006, on the first floor of Elliott when he heard something start rubbing the windows loudly. The vibrational noise went on and on and sounded like skin rubbing on the glass except very, very strong.

He looked out the window. Nobody was there. If a student had locked himself out and wanted to get in he would have banged on the window instead anyway.

Jeff checked outside the window the next day and found it was higher off the ground than he had expected (probably over five and a half feet). That ruled out a large dog getting on its hind legs and scratching the window. The window also didn't have any trees or other objects that would have rubbed against it. So, the only thing it could have been was someone wandering outside during the early hours of a Wednesday morning and deciding to rub the glass opportunistically when someone was right next to it. Possible, he supposed, but highly improbable, and he certainly hadn't seen anyone. Perhaps, though, it was something somewhat more inexplicable. Was it a ghost? It was pretty weird.

Emery Hall

The small, cute dormitory called Emery Hall was built to house nurses when the hospital was located at Hodgson Hall next door. It did not become a dorm for college students until 1976 when the hospital moved to its current location. The most recent of its many uses up until then was the hospital administration building. Downstairs, however, was the morgue.

When the first students moved in, the rooms of the former morgue were locked up tight. Rumor had it the autopsy table was still there. Everyone expected the building to be haunted. Unlike the former hospital, however, not much activity has been reported (to this author, anyway).

People who have lived there have reported a shadow figure moving around at will downstairs in the common area and kitchen but nothing upstairs where the living quarters are. I think this dorm needs some more investigation.

Gorgas Hall

James Veach sometimes comes to call
Over there at Gorgas Hall
He'll sit on your bed
While wrinkling your spread
And sometimes makes glass bottles fall.

Both Gorgas and Quintard were part of the Sewanee Military Academy campus until it merged with St. Andrew's in the early 1980's. One of the spirits seen out there was James Veach, who committed suicide in 1955. His story is included with the stories about the Cross.

Carla, who lived in Gorgas, had a ghost that kept visiting her room. She would make her bed up, go take a shower, and when she came back there would be impressions of someone sitting on her bed. Her room would get freezing cold in spots from time to time and she could often feel a presence with her. Several times she awoke to feel someone sleeping beside her in the bed but then there was no one there.

Carla had a picture she kept on her bedside table. She would set it up, turn around to do something else and when she looked at it again it would be turned face down. She did this many times and it would always get turned back face down. She finally just removed the picture from the table altogether.

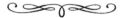

Nora and Cari were hanging out in their room in Gorgas. Nora was sitting on her bed. There was a shelf above her bed where she kept various things, including a whiskey bottle. She had the bottle tucked safely and securely at the back of the shelf. The bottle began to move. Both girls watched incredulously as it inched its way to the edge of the shelf. Though she attempted to move, she was not fast enough. The bottle came off the shelf and hit Nora in the head. She had the goose egg to prove that it really happened.

Nora was alone in the room one night. As she went to bed she saw the red glow from a mirror light. She wondered how it came on, but didn't think too much about it. She simply turned it off and went back to bed. As she got into bed, it came on again. She looked around and said, "Stop it, Gary," for they called their ghost Gary. At that point the light shone brighter. "Gary, I'm not dealing with this," she said, and the light turned all the way on.

Was James Veach or someone else a visitor to these rooms?

Hodgson Hall

The nurse down at Hodgson dorm
Thinks she's still in charge – her true form
Tucking some into bed
Chiding others instead
Best to follow her rules is the norm.

Hodgson rivals Tuckaway for the number of ghost stories associated with it. Built as a library in the 1880's, the building was turned into a hospital in 1900 and served as the only hospital between Chattanooga and Nashville for many years. It survived two fires, served thousands of patients, hosted the births of many, many babies, functioned as a training center for nurses, and boasted its own pediatric wing. When the hospital moved to its current location, the building and its annex (Emery) became a dormitory for several years. Then it was closed for a number of years before being renovated as a dorm. The predominant ghost is apparently that of a nurse with very strict beliefs, but there are reports of other specters as well.

Screaming

The first year Hodgson opened as a dorm (1976), it looked pretty much the same as it did as a hospital, with wide hallways, tall ceilings with old lights, huge windows, linoleum floors, and instructions on how to do artificial respiration in the emergency room-turned laundry room. It was kind of a scary place even on a good day.

Jackson was sleeping in one of his friend's rooms on the first floor. Julia was not there. He woke abruptly to see a figure standing just outside the window and screaming bloody murder. It did not really have a distinguishable shape, but he knew it was that of a woman. Frozen in fear, he could not move a muscle. This went on for about a minute that felt like an eternity. Jackson realized he HAD to stop it somehow, but felt he couldn't move or speak. With a monumental effort, he finally willed himself to say something and the figure disappeared.

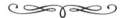

In the 1970's Maizey had a room on the second floor on the Southwest end, and was lucky enough to have her own bathroom. She never had any encounters with a ghost, but the week she went home to study for comps, she allowed a friend to stay there. Her friend was awakened one night by someone tugging on his feet, and opened his eyes to find a figure standing at the end of the bed. Yelling, he leapt out of bed and went running to the safety of the room of two other friends. It wasn't entirely safe, however, because one friend was sleeping "in the raw," and she was not happy to see him there in the middle of the night.

More on the Old Hospital

Having near narcoleptic episodes induced by calculus homework or having to write a French essay, Bernadette's senior year often featured afternoon naps in the sun in her corner room on the second floor of the Old Hospital. Her room was in an alcove next to a bathroom. She had a white board notepad on her door so folks could leave a message if they came by and missed her. Often while napping, she would hear footsteps come down the hall, pause, and then she would hear the pen scribbling on the notepad. She would get up to go to the door and say "Hey wait! I'm here!" only to open the door to an empty hall, and no note on the pad.

A Year's Worth of Haunting

The ghost visited Bernadette all the time. It took showers with her, tucked her in, sent bad dreams, got a little upset when the room was rearranged, and showed her disapproval of nighttime visitors. Once she saw fingers sliding around her head from behind. More than once she got freaked out and slept in the hall all night. She really did not like living in that room all year, and does not really like to talk about it, but is comforted to know there are so many other stories about the nurse ghost.

The Nurse

Many of the stories about Hodgson Hall include the spirit of a nurse. She is kind and motherly but also stern at times. She has often been encountered patrolling the halls and making sure her charges are following the rules.

One night the power went off in Hodgson and everyone gathered in the hallway to see what was going on. Someone saw a light coming towards them from the end of the hall. It got closer and closer. It was the figure of a nurse, holding a lantern. She said, "Everything is going to be okay." Then she turned and walked away.

On several occasions, Michael felt tugging on the bottom of his sheets and around his feet. Once it happened while the lights were still on and he saw the sheets move. When Stella told him there was supposed to be a nurse there who tucked people in, he said that made sense and that was what it seemed like.

Ariel couldn't sleep. She left her room in Hodgson to go down to the common room. While going down the hall she passed the figure of a nurse who put her finger to her lips while passing. When Ariel turned around to look again, the nurse had vanished.

Lots of people have encountered the nurse tucking them in at night, particularly the sheets around their feet. Two students, however, kept having the sheets around their feet neatly folded up around their ankles, leaving their feet uncovered.

Many have heard the sound of gurneys being pushed down the halls of the dorm.

In the Basement

When Seth was living in the basement of Hodgson, he woke up one night to see his closet door open by itself. He turned on the light and watched while it opened. The hair on the back of his neck prickled. He knew his roommate was asleep, so he figured it was a ghost.

Get Back to Bed!

One student was walking to the bathroom in the middle of the night, only to be stopped by a nurse in an old fashioned uniform. She told him, "You aren't allowed down this corridor! Patients are sleeping! Go back to your room!" He started to do as the nurse had told him when his brain kicked in. When he turned back around, she was gone.

Rachel saw the Hodgson nurse between 2 and 3 a.m. on July 19, 2006. She was rewriting her final paper for her English 101 class in summer school, and was sitting in the common room on the second floor at a large table under the old operating room light.

She was facing the wall on the downhill side of Hodgson when she noticed out of the corner of her eye a female figure dressed in white slowly moving down the stairs on the spiral staircase. When she looked directly at the staircase, the figure wasn't there. Rachel went back to work, thinking it must have just been fatigue. About ten minutes later, however, she saw the same form, this time standing still on the spiral staircase. Rachel was a little disturbed and went to bed. She was glad that summer school ended later that week, and she did not ever live in Hodgson again.

Ava's only experience with a ghost occurred when she lived in Hodgson during Summer School in 2005. She lived in a room on the top floor with a roommate. Late one night around three in the morning the door to their room opened and then closed. Ava was having a hard time sleeping so when it opened she sat up in bed and looked to see if it was her roommate. Her roommate, however, was in her bed asleep.

There was a floor length mirror propped against the wall close to the door and in it Ava saw the reflection of something white. There were no lights on in the room and all of their shades were down, so she couldn't figure out where the reflection came from. It was a large reflection and it stayed there for about thirty seconds. Ava was convinced the next day, and is still convinced, that it was the ghost of the nurse.

Not the Nurse

Some Hodgson stories are unrelated to the resident nurse. Two people who lived in a six-room suite on the top floor have seen the figure of a little boy in a flannel shirt crying in their common area.

Author's Note

A professor came to me after I gave a presentation of ghost stories. I had not mentioned the Hodgson stories. He asked if I had heard any stories of a little girl in white in Hodgson. I had not, but my daughter was there with me, and she had. "Was she looking for her doll?" she asked.

"Yes," he said. "When I was a student I lived in Hodgson and saw this little girl in a white nightgown one night in the corner of my room rummaging around. I actually threw a pillow at her." My daughter replied that she had heard several stories of this little girl, who supposedly died of scarlet fever. In those days people burned the belongings of those with the illness. The little girl wanted her doll back.

How many other former patients are still residents at Hodgson?

Hoffman Hall

If you'd really like to know why
Those bookshelves in Hoffman fly
Keep reading this tale
And it will unveil
The answer by and by.

Hoffman dormitory's history begins in Bridgeport, Alabama. The Hoffman Hotel was a first class hotel during the nineteenth century. After it closed in the 1880's, the building was dismantled, moved by train to Sewanee, and rebuilt. It was a five-story structure located approximately in the center of what is now University Avenue near the current Johnson dorm. Many organizations had group pictures taken sitting on the steep stairs of the building. Hoffman was the first "real dorm" in Sewanee. The students mostly lived in boarding houses presided over by refined women who had been widowed during the Civil War. When quality regulation of the boarding houses became difficult to oversee, the University turned toward the dormitory system. Mrs. Fannie Preston was the dorm's beloved matron for many years.

Hoffman was also the first University building (but not the last by any means) to burn. The current Hoffman was rebuilt after a fire in 1899. It is much smaller and plainer than its predecessor. The University Archives has some silverware and a silver tea service from the original Bridgeport Hotel.

Since a student told this story from the 1990's, more current students have come forward with similar recollections:

Meg lived in Hoffman. She knew that the chaplain had performed a blessing for her room a couple of years before she moved there. A lot of strange things had happened!

Deirdre, an intelligent and meticulous student, lived in the room during the first semester. She was well known around campus for her beautiful personality, but mostly for her brains! Nothing much happened to Deirdre (that she would admit, anyway) except that her tuition check, which she had left on her desk, vanished. Yes, we all misplace things, but not Deirdre and not a tuition check! She finally gave up looking for it. Then, when she was moving out of her room at the end of the semester, the check appeared on the top bookshelf. That could have been an honest mistake, though unlikely for Deirdre. It was not too scary, but it was just the beginning!

Meg moved into the room the following semester in January of 1995. At first just small things happened. Upstairs the girls were always rearranging their furniture and it was really hard to study. It almost seemed to become increasingly louder as the days went by. Meg's roommate Beatriz also noticed. This happened off and on the entire semester.

In the evenings there was a strange sound that was in the room. It sounded like someone slowly rubbing his hands together or moving his hands along the wall, except the sound was in the middle of the room or about a foot away from Meg's face. Again Beatriz also witnessed this. They would come home and the heat would be unbearable in their room that winter! Their personal cookware was hot to the touch and chocolate melted in their room. The more they laughed that it was a ghost, the worse things got!

One day Meg was trying to take a nap on a Sunday afternoon and Beatriz was studying. They lived on the first floor of Hoffman by the main entrance. Suddenly, the front door slammed open and hit the wall hard, startling Meg out of her nap. She had just enough time to say to Beatriz, "Did you hear that?" when she heard footsteps rapidly pounding down the hall as if they were coming straight to their room. As soon as the steps should have been at their door Meg's bookshelves flew off the wall and into the middle of the room. They did not fall down...they flew out of the wall! Beatriz never heard the door that sounded so loud to Meg, but she sure saw the bookshelves move. They changed their tune of making fun of the possibility of the ghost to recognizing it and asking it to leave them alone so they could all just get along. They did get along for the most part.

Over the next few weeks the bookshelf thing happened a few more times, no matter what was on it. The girls would acknowledge the ghost's presence and it would then leave them alone. Sometimes friends would visit and make fun of the ghost. On one occasion they had warned a friend not to make fun of it but he did not listen. Right after he made a comment an unopened bottle of champagne exploded.

Meg and Beatriz finally got sick and tired of the girls upstairs always rearranging their furniture. One night they went upstairs and knocked on their door while the girls were moving things around. To their surprise, no one answered the door. Meg and Beatriz knew they were in there! Several hours passed and finally they saw one of the students who lived in the room coming back from the library. She hadn't been home all day or night and she said she and her roommate had never rearranged their furniture!

The following year Meg lived in Emery and one of her former sorority sisters, Sierra, moved into her old room in Hoffman, which had become a single. Meg told her briefly about the room and advised her not to make fun of the ghost. She didn't think too much about it that semester. On the last day of the semester Meg ran into Sierra in line at lunch. Sierra apologized for thinking Meg was crazy for believing in ghosts.

The night before Sierra had been finishing up a term paper when the phone rang. She began talking with one of her friends about the end of the semester and she made a comment about how she was told that the room was haunted and that it was a crock. At that very instance her computer turned off and came right back on. In the middle of her paper were the words "FOOL, FOOL, FOOL." Sierra was thankful the year was nearly over. She developed great respect for the ghost.

Author's Note

More recently, I had this report about Hoffman: In Hoffman 26 there is a ghost that makes really odd sounds when you are in there by yourself. It sounds like someone rubbing her or his hands together.

Another student reported the constant sound of furniture being rearranged. It sounded as if it was coming from the attic. She and some others even went up to the attic to see what was there. There was no furniture there. Nevertheless, they continued to hear furniture moving in the attic.

The ghost is still there – twenty years later.

I also did some research for an Archives patron and found some interesting information about Hoffman in the process. The patron knew his stepbrother had attended Sewanee. As it turns out, his stepbrother, Gareth Moultrie Ward, of Memphis, died in a gun accident there in 1959 on the third floor of the dorm. He had stopped in his friend Danford Sawyer's room to admire a gun the student had just bought. Another boy was there as well. Sawyer took the bullets out and put them in a box. He was sitting on his bed looking at the gun when it discharged, hitting Ward in the chest and killing him. Apparently a bullet had been left in the chamber.

Is the ghost of Hoffman that of Gareth Moultrie Ward?

Hunter Hall

Hunter Hall was built in the 1950's on the site of the former Lovell house, a beautiful rambling wooden structure that had fallen into disrepair. The Lovell house served for many years as a boarding hall, so it saw a lot of activity in its heyday. It is named for its first owners, a family from Natchez, Mississippi who came to Sewanee early in its existence. Mrs. Lovell reportedly closed all her blinds and refused to watch when President Taft came past her house during his 1911 visit to Sewanee, because she would have nothing to do with a "Republican."

Hunter is one of the dorms built around the "study room" concept. The bedrooms on either end of each study room are so small that they are now singles instead of doubles, and the study room serves as a third bedroom.

Hunter's several ghost stories take place on both floors, in the hall bathrooms and even in the attic.

First, There is The Gentleman

On Suzette's first day at Sewanee, she was sleeping in her room, Hunter 12A. In the middle of the night she woke up feeling as if she were being watched. When she looked she saw a distinguished gentleman in a Sewanee gown standing over her bed looking at her. When Suzette turned on her bedside light, he vanished. It wasn't an evil feeling, just a confused one that he was not sure who she was or why she was in that bed.

The Ghosts of the Showers

Everything Genevieve and Tara experienced in Hunter revolves around the showers. They heard some friends of theirs in a room down the hall discussing their "haunted" shower, which was apparently the result (like many fictional Sewanee ghosts) of a suicide; they substantiated their claim by saying that the floor of their shower had been partially filled in with more concrete because the blood would not wash out. Their shower floor actually is higher than the standard Hunter shower, but the real reason is unknown; no suicides have taken place in Hunter or, as far as anyone knows, in the preexisting house. People may, however, have died of natural causes in the house.

As a joke and as part of a photography project, Genevieve and her roommates took pictures in the "haunted" shower. First, none of the negatives of that scene developed. They were all defective. Second, after taking those pictures of the shower down the hall, Genevieve and her roommates began noticing strange things while in their own shower! They would often hear knocking on the door or someone calling their names while showering, but nobody was knocking or yelling—Genevieve knows it wasn't a prank because she could see the door to the bathroom from her desk. Several times while her roommates experienced these events she witnessed that no one was near the bathroom. Genevieve also experienced voices and knocking, and all three of them described identical experiences.

Also, Genevieve heard that one of the girls in the original haunted shower room was locked in her bathroom one night at 2 a.m. She didn't lock the door; it just would not open. Apparently she was trapped for a while and got very frightened.

More Hunter Hauntings

A girl woke up one night in Hunter feeling as if someone was suffocating her with a pillow, but there was nothing there.

Several alumni and students have reported that the Hunter attic is haunted and sometimes you can hear the ghosts dancing and singing.

Hunter's Second Floor Bedfellow

Hilda lived on the second floor of Hunter during her sophomore year. One night she was having trouble falling asleep. After lying in bed for a while she heard her suitemate come into her room to get something from her closet, which was weird because it was late (after 2 a.m.). Hilda acted as if she were asleep (she thought that would be better than allowing her roommate to think she woke Hilda up, or getting into a conversation when she was so close to sleep). But Hilda never heard her door open again or heard anybody leave.

Thinking it was strange that her suitemate was just standing in her dark room, Hilda turned around to check it out. Nobody was there. Hilda decided that she must have been dreaming or that the wind blew the doors. She rolled back over. Then, as she tried to fall asleep, she felt someone getting into bed with her. Her heart skipping a beat, she leaned over and turned on her light. No one was there.

She looked to see if either of her suitemates was up, but to her surprise her door had been locked the whole time so nobody could have come in - unless they were still there! She searched her room (which was not very big or conducive to hiding so it didn't take very long) and found nobody.

She unlocked the door to find both her suitemates asleep in their beds. She re-locked her door (even though that clearly made no difference), and went to sleep with the lights on. It was just too creepy and unexplainable to be merely a dream.

Johnson Hall

The ghost at Johnson's a girl
With long brown hair and no curl.
She'll knock boys down
Those stairs to the ground
And take form as a light like a pearl.

Johnson Hall is on University Avenue at the site of an old boarding house last presided over by a woman named Mrs. Galleher. It stood next door to the Kirby-Smith house, Powhattan. When her house burned, Mrs. Galleher remarked stoically that at least she had had the house when she needed it.

If you look at Johnson Hall and Cannon Hall on South Carolina Avenue you can tell that the same architect designed both of them. Both dorms have floor plans that feature rooms of many sizes and shapes. Originally the two dorms were going to be built next to each other, with Cannon on the site of an older dorm, Hoffman, that burned. Cannon ended up on South Carolina after a residence burned, leaving a site available. It has now been completely renovated and has a new dorm connected to it. Johnson, on the other hand, remains one of the few living spaces that have not had a facelift in many, many years. Women haunt both dorms, but the two spirits are from different centuries.

The ghost of Johnson, when seen, has always been a girl with long brown hair. She has been noticed on the stairs to the basement and to the third floor, in rooms on the first and second floor, and particularly in a certain room, one with four roommates, on the third floor. The story around town is that the ghost is that of a former student, but this has not been confirmed. Perhaps it was a guest of Mrs. Galleher. There are stories about other dorms (particularly McCrady) of a girl with long brown hair. Does this ghost haunt more than one place? Did it live at one time in both dorms? Was it a resident of or visitor to Sewanee? These are questions that simply cannot be answered.

Room 25

Hilary was once a proctor at Johnson Hall. She lived in room 25. In October of that year she was lying in bed mostly asleep one morning around five-thirty when she felt someone sit on the end of the bed. The bed squeaked and the mattress moved down. She woke up, scared someone was in her room (and in her bed!), but when she got the courage to open her eyes, she saw that no one was there. Her mom called less than a minute later to tell her that her favorite uncle had passed away.

Johnson, First Floor

Megan reported that she witnessed her first floor room door open and close by itself and felt someone sit on the end of her bed. She then heard from several others that this is a common occurrence in the dorm.

When Shala was living in Johnson on the first floor she and her roommate noticed that if they left the door ajar, it would regularly open and close by itself. When they asked the older students about it, they said it's been happening for a number of years, but no one knows why. It was especially annoying to Shala that she would leave the door open to go to the bathroom, only to find herself locked out when she tried to get back in.

Stories of the Brown-Haired, Green-Eyed Female Spirit of Johnson circa 1989-2009

Teresa lived in the only true quad on campus, a third-floor Johnson suite (room 47). Even though it was haunted she managed to live there for two years with two of the same roommates. There was definitely another presence in their room. Many odd things happened over those two years. One of Teresa's roommates insisted that there was an evil presence in the room. She had really bad nightmares and would come wake Teresa up to crawl into her bed. She ended up leaving Sewanee right before Spring Break and from the first day back on campus after break Teresa and her other two roommates started having the same types of nightmares. Their new roommate the next year had stayed with them some the previous year after their other roommate had left and even she was very spooked. She disliked sleeping in the room alone, and Teresa did her best NOT to be the last one in bed at night because in the dark she often felt smothered or recognized a presence standing next to her bed. All of them experienced their printers turning themselves on in the middle of the night several times.

She is About 5'8" Tall

Laurie, one of Teresa's roommates, experienced much more than Teresa. She witnessed a spirit there who was around 5'8" with brown hair and green eyes, but who didn't manifest herself in completely human form. All the roommates felt her presence both in the room and on the stairs going to the laundry room in the basement. The ghost does not like men, as she accosted a male friend of theirs in the hallway. Some believe that the spirit was a student who was assaulted in the basement by a man back in the 70's. Although there have been incidents of assault in Johnson in the past, no student died as the result of an attack.

Laurie thought the ghost was especially creepy because she would sit on the bookshelf over Laurie's bed and watch her quite often. That ghost, at least according to Laurie and Teresa, was around in the third floor room all year both years they lived there. They often saw her hovering over one of the beds or sitting on a bed. Sometimes she was an orb of light that floated around. She would float over their shoulders to watch them study, and they could feel her touching them. She would sit on their computers or simply hover.

More than one girl felt she was pushed down the basement stairs when she went down to do laundry — always from the same stair, the fourth from the bottom. It was always a cold spot, too. Sometimes she came into the shower with students. She became known as "ghost girl."

She Doesn't Like Boys Very Much

A male friend of the women in Room 47 was on the stairs, which are just inside the front door. He was going to scare his friends so he called them from his cell phone to tell them he was locked out of the dorm in order to get them to come out of their room. For those alumni who remember that dorms were always open and unlocked until late at night, know that now they are locked all of the time. Students open them with their ID cards in most places. Also, most dorms are coed. Monitored sign-ins to dorms are a foreign concept to current students.

This student had gotten into the dorm already but wanted them to believe he was waiting outside so that when they came out of their room he could scare them and catch it all on his cell phone camera. He was headed up the stairs with video going when all of a sudden the spirit girl whooshed past him and gave him a shove, and he fell down the stairs.

Right then the girls came out of their room. "Did you see that!" he yelled. "I just got pushed downstairs by a ghost!" He seemed to know that the spirit had long brown hair. Amazingly, his cell phone caught the whole thing, depicting a spirit figure rushing past him and him tumbling down the stairs. I guess the joke was on him!

Not Just For Sewanee's College Students

During Sewanee's summer music program during the late 1980's a girl who lived in a top floor private room was plagued by middle-of-the-night happenings. Her light would come on, or her radio. There is a more vivid account of this on the internet, but I could not locate the author, so chose not to relate this in detail. A Google search will turn it up for you if you're interested. It's interesting to mention, however, because it demonstrates that this lore is not simply passed among college students year to year. The person relating that story had no relation to the college other than through a summer program.

Outside Johnson

Mildred was driving one afternoon to a meeting. Just at the point between the Phi house on the corner of Texas and University and Johnson Hall, she saw Mrs. Holland strolling along the way. Suddenly she thought she should stop to pick her up, for certainly she was going to the same meeting. She did stop alongside the figure. She made the polite gestures of asking Mrs. Holland to ride with her, when the figure vanished. It was at that point that Mildred recalled that Mrs. Holland had passed away a number of years before.

Lambda Chi Alpha House

The Lambda Chi Alpha house is an "A" frame fraternity house on Mitchell Avenue. Built in the 1960's or early 1970's, it is new compared to many of the other fraternity houses on campus.

Patrick knows that Lambda Chi Alpha is haunted because he has had first-hand experience with the spirits there. In the fall of 2007 he returned a little early to school. Since the dorms weren't open, he stayed in his fraternity house for a few days.

One night Patrick was in the upper common room sleeping on a couch when he woke up to the sound of footsteps. Thinking it was one of his friends he sat up a bit to see that not only were the lights on when they hadn't been before but there also were two women he didn't know in the room. One was over him bent down as if she was trying to check up on him and the other was walking through one of the back upper doors out to the back balcony. Then she went over the balcony and back in through the opposite door.

Patrick rubbed his eyes as he asked why these women were here and at that point they disappeared. He is not the only one who has encountered the noises and a presence in that room.

McCrady Hall

McCrady's ghost, I confess
Is a girl in a purple dress
She's relatively tame
And yet all the same
Her presence makes people a mess.

McCrady was the first dorm in Sewanee to become a "co-ed" dorm, in the 1970's, and it was quite scandalous at the time. Boys lived in one wing and girls in the other. They shared a common room. Now most dorms on campus are co-ed.

McCrady dorm is located on the site of the former McCrady family home and is part of the walking campus on the Alabama Avenue side of town.

Louise experienced a ghost in McCrady on her third night in Sewanee. She escorted a visitor of hers to the door. As she walked back into the left side door, she looked across to the glass of the back door. A reflection showed a young lady with long brown hair and a purple ¾-length skirt sitting on what should have been the steps in front of her. When she turned to look, there wasn't a girl sitting on the steps.

More on the Girl With Brown Hair Dressed in Purple

I had collected that story of McCrady when I first started asking for stories to tell at a Halloween party at the Archives. On Halloween that year, 2007, the Archives building was open for trick or treating and for a ghost story event. One woman came with her son, and she started talking about how creepy it could get working as a custodian in the University buildings. She mentioned that her first encounter with a spirit was in McCrady Hall, a woman with long brown hair dressed in purple! That was the first time I got two similar stories about the same place from people who did not know each other.

Since then several people have mentioned seeing "the woman in purple with long brown hair" walking the halls of McCrady.

In October of 2013 I was invited to tell stories at the college's Community Engagement house. One of the hosts had been in the front yard during story time hosting another activity. As I was leaving, she came in and asked her friend, "Did she say anything about a girl with brown hair and a purple dress in McCrady?" Spooky!

An Encounter With Francesca (a real spirit, trust me!)

One semester Clara took an art class for which she spent some time in the cemetery trying to draw the graves. Interestingly, she happened to pick one of the spirits there. Her name was Francesca. Many nights Clara used to pass through the cemetery to reach her dorm (McCrady) after a long and trying day at art lab.

One night she came back from her art lab very tired and went to bed at around 2 a.m. Very soon afterward something spooky started to happen. She heard the shower turn on. She asked her suite mates and her roommate about it the next day, and found out that no one was using the shower during that time.

The next day something very weird happened. She turned off her computer and went to bed at 1 a.m. She locked her door that day because her roommate was not there. Suddenly, at about 3 a.m., her computer automatically opened and the sudden sound woke Clara up. The events started repeating, and she began to realize that she was hanging around with Francesca too much in the cemetery. As long as she lived in McCrady she heard noises of

93

someone knocking on the door after she went to bed. Francesca was waiting for her. Is she still there?

Another McCrady Story

Cheryl and her roommate Victoria moved into the basement of McCrady (in the 1980's), and in decorating the room, Victoria hung a plaque on a hook on the wall. From the start the plaque refused to stay on the wall. This hook was almost closed, and there was no way for the decoration to fall or slide - it would have to be lifted off the hook and dropped. It would fall when they were there, when they were not there, and when they were asleep. The final straw, after three weeks of this, came one day when Clara was in the room alone. She was standing at the desk where the plaque was located, and she turned to walk away. The plaque fell. She whipped around, went back and picked up the plaque, and tugged on the still secure hook. Then she told her roommate when she got back that the plaque was not to go up again.

Clara and Victoria also noticed a smell that occurred off and on in one corner - a rotten odor as if something had died. It sure rattled their nerves having the plaque jump off the hook all hours of the day and night till they quit hanging the thing on the wall.

Phillips Hall

Phillips Hall was built as a dormitory for nurses at the nursing school. It has mostly served as a women's dorm, with a short stint as the French House.

Although there are many rumors of ghost stories involving Phillips, there are only a few brief ones to tell. Residents have complained of furniture dragging around and random knocking on doors.

One summer during the Bridge summer program, which was housed in Phillips, several students and the head resident witnessed the light in the attic come on, go off, and come on again. They had the police check it out. The door to the attic was locked. There was nothing up there to trip the motion detector lights. Others have seen this phenomenon throughout the years.

Quintard Hall

Quintard, built in 1899, was the first dormitory for students in the Sewanee Military Academy, then called the Sewanee Grammar School. Before then the high school students lived in boarding houses with "those bad influences," the college boys.

In 1919 a fire completely gutted the inside. The severity of the fire, which was intentionally set, was compounded by the presence of the ammunition room in the building. The preparatory department moved to Palatka, Florida, while the dorm was rebuilt. Now Quintard houses students of the University. This is one of the dorms from which SMA students could see James Veach walking the cross road at night (see the story on the Cross for the full account of James Veach).

All the stories collected here happened after the year 2000. They are short, but do not necessarily point to just one ghost at the dorm, or even to Mr. Veach.

Tim was taking an experimental film class. One day he decided to make a film from the roof of Quintard, which is flat and all gravely. He was up there by himself, and heard footsteps close by in the gravel, but nobody was there.

Elaine had an encounter on the first floor. She was in the bike room getting her bike to go to class. No one lives on the first floor except the head resident, so during the middle of the day it is pretty much deserted. When she went into the bike room, she kept feeling as if she was seeing someone out of the corner of her eye. She dismissed it and went on to class. When she came back from class, she was putting her bike up and kept getting that same sensation of getting a glimpse of someone in her peripheral vision, but when she looked, no one was there. When she opened the door to come out into the hall after putting her bike away, Elaine saw someone walking towards her, and was very sure this time that there actually was a tall male figure right beside her, but when she turned to look squarely at whoever it was, no one was there. She went upstairs quickly to seek the comfort of more people.

One night Shelley and her roommate were in their room on the second floor of Quintard and Shelley's radio would not turn off. She unplugged it and pulled out the batteries and it kept playing and playing for about half an hour. Shelley and her roommate were both there, and they checked repeatedly for the absence of any kind of power source, and they were both stone cold sober. They still have no idea how that was even possible.

St. Luke's Hall

St. Luke's Hall is one of the very first stone buildings erected on campus, through the generosity of a British benefactor, Mrs. Charlotte Manigault. She asked to name it St. Luke's Hall in honor of Vice-Chancellor and Bishop of Tennessee Charles Todd Quintard, who was also a medical doctor and a member of the Society of St. Luke the Physician. Her gift also included a large collection of scholarly religious works. St. Luke's was built to be the theological department, and remained the seminary until 1983 when the seminary moved to the campus of the former Sewanee Military Academy. At various times St. Luke's has housed the seminary classrooms, the theological library, a bookstore, the student radio station (WUTS), the Music and English departments, the Sewanee Review, a small performance space, an oratory, and student rooms. Each renovation has preserved the original look of the exterior building. Its space is now devoted entirely to dormitory space.

Sharon lived in St. Luke's on the fourth floor for the spring semester of 2007. Her roommate from the previous semester had gone abroad, and she was living with another friend on the fourth floor (room 413). One night her roommate, who was a very sound sleeper, had already gone to sleep and Sharon was in bed and almost asleep when she heard someone knock on the door. She got up and checked, and there was no one in the hall. She thought it was odd, but figured she was half asleep and hearing things.

The next day Sharon was alone in the room in the bathroom getting ready. She had the door to the bathroom open because her boyfriend was going to come over. She heard knocking again and went quickly to answer the door. This time she was fully awake. Again, there was no one there. She didn't hear anyone in the hall, or any doors opening or closing. It would have been impossible for someone to reach another room or a hiding place in such a short time. After that, sporadically when she was the only one in the room she would hear knocking on the wooden dresser or the bathroom door. She could never find a reasonable explanation for the knocking, no matter how hard she looked or thought about the situation.

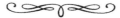

There used to be a ghost in St Luke's in the classroom next to the Blue Box, a small performance area, who would push the door open and shut at unexpected times. Carly used to joke that it was following her, because the same year she had Latin class in that room, she also seemed to have a ghost of the same variety in her dorm room.

One night three separate people felt a presence in their rooms, and each told the same person the next day. Stan felt that someone was standing over him, but no one was there. Several times Kent's radio suddenly blasted out static and noise.

On November 5, 1920 the college newspaper headline read, *Gruesome Ghost Infests Suite Three, St. Luke's*. Mysteriously, the page on which the story was supposed to continue was missing from the paper. No other copies of that issue could be located. Is it the same spook, revived after a long nap?

Trezevant Hall

Trezevant dorm was originally called "New College" dorm and was part of a vision to build a second college campus for women. Instead, the college went co-ed. Trezevant rooms are suites with doors opening onto a central courtyard.

Phoebe, a resident of Trezevant, and a few of her friends played hide and go seek in the University Cemetery one evening. During the course of the night, she lost her wallet among the graves. She spent the entire next day searching for it, but was never able to find it. That night when she returned to her room she found her wallet lying there right in the middle of her bed. As soon as she noticed it she felt something rush by her and close the door. It was not her roommate or suitemates because she immediately checked outside and nobody was there. So that was that; she had her wallet and is convinced that a ghost returned it to her. She made great connections with a ghost that night.

Trezevant's Tragic Ghost

At the beginning of the school year in 2001 a student was killed in a tragic off-campus accident. Although he lived in Cannon Dorm, he had a lot of friends in Trezevant. For the first few months after his death, he could be seen just lingering and watching his friends, presumably to make sure they were okay.

Tuckaway Dorm

Tuckaway's poltergeist ghost,
Well, he likes hazing the most.
Locking students inside
Their rooms while they tried
To get out is his favorite boast.

Tuckaway has so many stories attached to it, I'd like to begin with this response from a student: "I live in Tuckaway 306, the 'haunted room,' and let me assure you my roommate and I have seen some things."

Although room 306 is the central place of ghostly activity in Tuckaway, the ghost's (or ghosts') antics are not confined to that room. That room has been reconfigured since the 1970's and was even was closed off for a while. The ghost, however, apparently had plenty of time to kill, maybe sticking around in 306 while the room was closed or perhaps haunting others who just haven't said anything yet.

Tuckaway sits on the corner of Tennessee Avenue and Arkansas, a quaint rock dorm made of pick-up stone with meandering corridors and a wide, comfortable front porch. It's easy to see that it once served as an Inn. The long main room just inside the door has been a dining hall, art gallery, and large reception room, and now is a living room for the dorm.

The building, built in 1930, is named for Miss Johnnie Tucker, beloved long-time matron of Tuckaway and owner of the boarding house that previously sat on the site (the Cotten House, which burned in 1926 while Miss Johnnie was out of town). This dorm and the previous house saw many students and other visitors, including Tennessee Williams' grandfather, the Rev. Walter Dakin. It was a hub for social activity in earlier times, especially dancing, Sewanee's favorite pastime of the day (besides baseball).

Tuckaway's ghost stories span from the 1960's to the present. The rumors that have grown from the stories hint that three students have committed suicide in the dorm, but there is no reliable evidence pointing to any deaths in Tuckaway.

First Mention of the Tuckaway Ghost

Gary lived in one of the rooms adjacent to the "Fishbowl," the common area just inside the front doors of Tuckaway. One evening he was at home studying at his desk. All of a sudden something compelled him to look up. When he did he saw a spectral woman in antiquated garb pass through his door — but only from the torso up. She disappeared, and he jumped up and ran out of the room. He couldn't have seen that, could he? It felt so real — or rather, surreal. He decided he wouldn't tell anyone, as he could visualize the teasing that would occur for months after. Just as he had convinced himself that he had NOT really seen anything at all, Jim came running up from the common room directly underneath; he had seen legs disappearing into the ceiling. When the word got out, as it usually does in Sewanee, Gary and Jim discovered they were not the only ones who had seen this phenomenon.

In fact, similar stories have surfaced many times, told by students, visitors, faculty, and staff. They report that others have seen multiple, partial apparitions milling about the ground floor of Tuckaway dressed in mid-nineteenth century garb. The ghosts always appeared in the early evening (7 to 10 p.m.) and only their torsos were visible in the main living room because the other halves of their spectral bodies appeared to extend down into the floor. Those in the basement common room could see their legs and feet. The Cotten house had had a ground floor a few feet lower than the floor level of the dorm.

That story was actually the "official" Tuckaway ghost story told by the historiographer and others in the 1970's, but the students involved in this particular incident were in school in the early 2000s.

He's a Mischievous Ghost

Austin was hanging out in his friend's room in Tuckaway on the second floor. They were sitting around talking, and suddenly the window flew open. He went over to close it, and had some trouble. He was literally putting all of his strength into closing that window and it wouldn't budge. Finally it closed, and he locked it, and after that it flew open again. It was CREEPY!!!!

A woman relayed that her husband awoke one night in the middle of the night with a grey smoky figure standing in his doorway. He knew instantly that this figure was there to harm him. When the figure began to move towards him in the bed, he literally called on the name of Jesus and told the ghost to leave. Thankfully, it listened.

The First Account of the Tuckaway 306 Ghost

One year there was a special Friday evening of Sewanee ghost stories at the Chi Psi house with one of the English professors, himself a former student. He had dressed up like Dracula in a tuxedo, long black cape, red sash, and iron cross medallion hanging below his bow tie.

He shared a number of really interesting stories with the audience that night. In particular, he shared his own experience with the Tuckaway Ghost. He said that when he lived in Tuckaway, he had a suite with three other guys, one that had the main center study room with two side bedrooms configuration. He was studying one afternoon in the center room with the door closed and locked from the inside. There was no other way into the suite other than the door he was sitting near. The door to his bedroom was shut and the window inside the bedroom shut and locked. No one else was in the suite. Suddenly, he heard a loud

WHUMP! He went into his bedroom, and opened the closet. ALL of his clothes were on the floor of the closet, but all of the hangers were still hanging motionless on the rod.

The room has since been reconfigured into a double. You can still see vestiges of how the room used to be. One person related: About the outline of the door in the wall, we could hear knocking at the old door when no one was in the hallway.

More Stories from Tuckaway 306

Nicholas lived in Tuckaway 306. He stated that there is supposed to be a pentagram under the carpet. (That's unverified, but it sounds good. That's how rumors spring up around stories.) He was getting ready to go to sleep. His roommate was out of town. He turned all of the lights off. Just as he was getting comfortable in his bed, his roommate's bedside lamp turned on. Nicholas shuffled over and turned it off. As he got back to his warm bed, it happened again. After a few more times of that, Nicholas gave up and left the lamp on for the night.

If you look at the door to room 306 you can see cut marks below the doorknob, and tell that the doorknob is new. Naturally, there is a story behind that.

Jan Drake-Lowther was head resident at Tuckaway for a number of years. She was well loved by the students, and very down to earth. She explained why the room had a new door handle. I (the author) brought a group of second graders over to hear her ghost story, and she took us up to "the room" on the third floor and showed us the new doorknob to that room, then related the story of what happened there. The student living there was getting ready to go to a formal. He came back from the community bathroom down the hall. When he went to leave his room again, he found that his door would not open. He appeared to be locked in his room (which is supposedly impossible because the doors don't lock from the inside). He called to his proctor, who came with the master key. The master key would not open the door. He went to get Miss Jan. HER key would not open the door. They called the police, who were reluctant to go so far as to break the door down. They tried

104

removing the hinges. That didn't help. When Physical Plant Services came, they tried the doorknob. The whole apparatus fell out of the door, but the door STILL would not open. All this time (several hours by now) the poor student was stuck inside. What must his date have been thinking! Finally, a Physical Plant worker broke through the door. You can see that the door has had a new handle installed.

The NEXT year in Tuckaway, Miss Jan did the room assessments at the beginning of the year. She evaluated each room to note any damage so that students would not be charged at the end of the year for damage that existed before they moved in. When she gave her reports to her proctor, one was missing. Guess which one it was! So the proctor did another assessment of room 306. At the registration tent, guess which packet was the ONLY one missing. You guessed it! The key to the room was missing as well.

When Roger lived in Tuckaway, his friend lived in "the room" on the third floor. One night Roger heard him yelling and pounding on his door and went up to investigate. His friend was yelling, "Let me out!" This is after the new doorknob was installed. The door does not lock from the inside. Roger couldn't open the door. He ran down and got Miss Jan and she came with her master key and unlocked the door from the outside.

Luis, another former room 306 occupant, had his clothes thrown about and the dresser drawers opened in the middle of the night — more than once. Henry saw a spectral figure sitting by his desk. Patterson woke up to find a figure above him that he felt was malicious.

George and Tucker roomed together one year in Tuckaway 306. One night they were getting to sleep when somebody said "GOOD NIGHT." George thought it was Tucker so he made some comment about it. After a moment of silence, Tucker replied that he thought it had been George talking. Another time, something woke George up in the middle of the night and when he looked across the room at his computer, there was a shadow sitting at his desk looking at the screen. When George moved, it got up and walked through the closed door of the room.

Joe had a ghost that lived in his room in Tuckaway who would go around and close doors if he had left them open or turn off the lights or radio. He was a very energy efficient ghost.

Clark reported that he had a creepy vibe from room 306 early on. He quickly accepted the ghost as a kind of third roommate and then didn't think about it very much.

Several other students admitted getting the feeling of another presence in that room when they were alone.

Alan and Rick lived in Tuckaway 306 their sophomore year. They would see a person standing behind them in the reflection of their computer screen and turn around to find no one there. When they looked back to their screen, the ghost's face was right there in the screen as if it was standing over their shoulders. Once Alan was taking a nap only to be awakened with the ghost sitting on his chest, its face inches from his own. That is not a good way to wake up from a nice nap.

On Terry's first night as a resident of "the haunted" room, he heard scratching coming from the inside of his closet. It was loud enough to wake him. At times, during the first two months or so he saw three white, purple, and orange globes that floated around the room, glowing.

Terry's roommate bought a brand new TV. The two of them thought it was defective because the volume would shoot up at random times. One day Terry was playing a video game on it and the volume keep going up, and after turning it back down a couple times he looked around the room and yelled, "Stop turning the goddamn volume up!" Immediately the volume went back to his original settings. He never had that problem again. He had a radio alarm clock that was always set on the school's radio channel, WUTS. One day when the Terry and his roommate were sitting in the room the radio out of nowhere turned on and began scrolling through channels. This radio normally required a person to turn a wheel to change stations. They chalked that antic up to the ghost.

When Kazi and Olsen lived there they were never able to open the windows. Then one day they came in and the windows were wide open and they could not shut them.

One day the power went out in that room alone.

Workmen were fixing something in that room one day. They left for lunch and when they come back the room was freezing cold. The AC was not on.

As a first semester freshman Allan had a very quiet roommate named Gordon. One night Allan came in late from the library and went to bed. He assumed Gordon was asleep. All of a sudden the door was slammed open against the closet door. Allan woke with a start. He could hear someone stumbling around the room as if drunk. Then the guy started scratching his skin. This would have been a strange thing for Gordon to do but Allan figured that's who it was. The next morning when he woke up, Gordon wasn't there. He came in a little later with bags in his hands. He had gone home for two days.

Lots of students and alums alluded to other stories about room 306 but did not give specifics. Suffice it to say the spirit of room 306 is somewhat of a poltergeist.

Some Stories From "The Attic"

There is another area of Tuckaway also plagued by spirits.

On the fourth floor there are only three rooms. They are misshapen, low-ceilinged, and kind of eerie. When Nigel first saw these rooms his freshman year, he expressed his fascination with them. He was told by an upperclassman that he shouldn't try to live there because those rooms were "haunted."

Nevertheless, he eventually came to live in Tuckaway 402. Quite a few times that year he heard banging sounds coming from the ceiling directly above the bed. It was as if someone was up there stomping. It was loud, and right over his bed. The room was in the eaves and had no attic. This happened often, usually around one or two in the morning. Nigel started making a shrine, but it did not do any good.

Note: This room was one of the rooms where I stopped with my group of elementary school kids, and after the student related his story to them, the ghost stopped his hanky-panky.

The Ghost on the Fire Escape

The year Trammell was proctor at Tuckaway, he had a complaint from a senior who was living in the attic, that somebody was banging and making a lot of noise on the door by the fire escape. He ran very quickly to let them in and get them quiet, but nobody could be found. His fellow proctor also reported the noise. The Head Resident told them she wakes up whenever someone climbs the fire escape and that night she did not wake up. That day, while making rounds Trammell sprinkled holy water on every door.

There are probably lots more stories out there about Tuckaway. I am just waiting for them to get back to me. Maybe you will be one of those with a new story to tell.

Outdoor Spaces

Cowan Highway

There have been some ghostly sightings on the Cowan highway. A Confederate soldier has been seen on the side of the road on 41A at the base of the mountain.

Ten thousand or more Union and Confederate troops came over the Mountain during the Civil War, mostly up the Breakfield Road through Decherd or the old Cowan Road. They could, however, have come up one of several other routes as well, or come home to Cowan or Winchester from many routes. Some were not far from where the Cowan Road now lies. Ghosts are not always tied to the places they died. There is no official documentation confirming Confederate deaths in the area. The only official records include a few injuries in the Battle of Sewanee, and that was a skirmish on top of the Mountain.

Who is the Confederate apparition at the bottom of the Mountain?

Green's View

The University has three lookouts within a mile of the central campus of the University. One of them, Green's View, is named for founder William Mercer Green, who had a house near the bluff before the Civil War. Incendiaries burned most of the houses on campus in 1862, so Bishop Green rebuilt closer to the main campus after the war. Green's View looks out into Rowark's Cove, a beautiful farming community. Far away you can see the waters gleaming off Woods Reservoir. It can be the perfect place to stargaze. It is no wonder a spirit hangs around this area.

Iris, a former Sewanee student, related an experience she and her friend had there at night. She had always felt a huge difference between taking a walk out to the Cross alone at night and taking a walk out to Green's View. In fact, she would never walk out to Green's View alone. It gave her a very creepy feeling of being watched from the woods, and something menacing coming closer and closer.

Once in her senior year, Iris and her friend were driving around in Iris' car and they decided to go look at the stars from

Green's View. She did not say anything to her friend of her feelings about the place, and Iris hoped that maybe since they were kind of punchy and in a car that it would be a different experience. The night sky was very clear and the stars were plentiful and amazing. They sat silently gazing for a while, and sure enough, Iris started to get the creepy feeling that they were not safe, and something was closing in on them from the woods.

They had not been talking about anything creepy, and Iris had never expressed an interest or a belief in anything supernatural, so she was surprised that suddenly her friend exclaimed, "OK, let's get out of here!" Iris asked her if she felt something, and she acknowledged the same looming menacing feeling that Iris did.

One night a group of students sat out at Green's View looking at the stars and listening to Mozart. When the piece ended there was suddenly a noise like someone rubbing against a bass guitar string. It sounded very eerie. A malevolent feeling crept up on the group. Needless to say, they left in a hurry.

Tessa remembered that in her freshman year she was walking out to Green's View at night, and on the way back met up with a professor who escorted her back to campus, then suddenly disappeared. On another occasion, the same thing happened to another student: he appeared, escorted her back and then disappeared. This supports an earlier legend of a "perambulating professor" who reportedly would appear to students on the road, put his arm around them and walk with them, then suddenly vanish. He liked to wear slippers and make shuffling noises while walking with someone.

Though Iris has never encountered the ghost of the professor, she believes that there is something malevolent out there at Green's View and that the professor's spirit protects lone walkers from whatever that energy is.

Mitchell Avenue Outside Hunter

It was December 13, 1982, and the first snow of the season. Rebecca and Betsy had borrowed some trays from Gailor (the former dining hall) in order to go sledding. It was about 11:30 in the evening. They were about to sled down the street off of University Avenue that goes right past Hunter dorm (Mitchell Avenue). Rebecca saw a man at the bottom of the hill, but this was no ordinary man. His head was quite large, and glowed like the moon. The only visible features on his face were dark hollows for his eyes. He appeared to be wearing a dark cloak. He looked up at them with his head cocked at an odd angle, as if perhaps his neck were broken. In fact, it gave the appearance that he was maybe hanging from a noose.

Rebecca couldn't believe what she was seeing. She kept trying to get up the courage to sled down the hill. Finally, she said to Betsy, "Do you see something at the bottom of the hill?"

Betsy said, "Yes, I do."

Rebecca replied, "I think we're seeing a ghost."

"I think you're right."

They walked away calmly until they were about fifty yards away, then they broke into screams and ran to their own dorm (Cleveland). They woke up Rebecca's friend's roommate and got her spooked. They all stayed up for several hours just being terrified.

The next night, Rebecca and Betsy took reinforcements and went back to the scene at the same hour. There was no sign of anything like what they saw; there were no weird reflections or optical illusions. They looked for tracks in the snow where the man had been, but found none. They even researched whether someone had hanged himself in that vicinity, but such information was not available.

Was it a one-time event, or has it perhaps happened to others? It is best to play it safe and be prudent when traveling Mitchell Avenue at night. After all, ghosts have been reported in the nearby dorm, Hunter, and in the Lambda Chi house just up the street, as well as in several other nearby buildings.

Old Farm Road

Old Farm Road is just what you would expect – a road that led to the old farm, which operated from 1900-1950. There is now a new farm operating out beyond Old Farm Road. The road itself is now full of houses on one side and a practice football field on the other, though there are some garden plots for a lucky few leaseholders.

Sylvia had the dickens frightened out of her when she was walking down Old Farm Road. Suddenly a big figure in white came running hard right after her. Before it reached her, it vanished!

Sewanee Memorial Cross

When my friends and I were young, we rode a bus each summer from Memphis to Monteagle to get to Camp Gailor-Maxon at the DuBose Conference Center. When we could finally spot the fifty-five foot tall concrete-on-stone Cross from the highway, we knew we were close enough to start getting excited.

The Sewanee Memorial Cross graces a Southwestern brow of the mountain where it has stood tall since 1923 as a memorial to fallen soldiers of Franklin County and the University. The cornerstone was laid on Armistice Day of 1922. The engineering students designed it, and the entire town came to help clear the land and lay the first stones. Community members cut the rock base, and women brought the picnic. The Sewanee Military Academy students marched down singing hymns. At 11 a.m. everyone stopped for a period of silence and a prayer.

For a long time the main highway was routed right by the Cross. In fact, the road now called Tennessee Avenue, which presently ends at the Cross was called University Avenue until the two names were switched in the 1950's. You can still see remnants of the road leading to the Cowan Highway (41A), which was blocked off in the 1980's.

The Cross remains a favorite place for a morning walk, a view of the sunset, picnics, and even throwing bread crumbs for the bats to swoop down and catch. It is at the end of a straight, narrow road of several rolling hills flanked by native trees. One side now has an accompanying walking path in the woods beside the road.

The cluster of dorms near the beginning of the road used to be part of the Sewanee Military Academy before the preparatory school merged with St. Andrew's to become St. Andrew's-Sewanee School in the 1980's. Two of the buildings, Quintard and Gorgas, were used as dormitories and are still used for that purpose by the College.

Naturally, there must be some ghost stories attached to this mystical place.

Veach

James Veach was an SMA student who committed suicide shortly after returning from Christmas break in 1955. He bought a length of rope and went and hanged himself in the woods on the Lost Cove trail from the Sherwood Road entrance. After it was discovered that Veach was missing, search parties formed to go look for him, only to be halted due to one of Sewanee's many thick fogs. He was not found until the next day.

His best friend, University honor student William Boone Massey, subsequently fatally shot himself. Upon hearing about his friend, Massey became very upset. He left a note for his roommate asking not to be awakened in the morning. He lived in Gailor Hall, which at that time was the school's refectory and a dormitory. Some time during the day, a Gailor worker heard a gunshot. Soon afterwards Massey was found in a friend's room. He had gone there, gotten his friend's gun, and shot himself. Two tragic suicides, and the only two ever publicly reported, although one other was recounted in a letter found in the Archives in Sewanee.

In 2008 an acquaintance of Massey allowed that the two boys had been lovers, and that others had found this out. In 1955 this was scandalous. Had the social climate been different, this double tragedy could have been prevented.

There have been reports from both SMA alums and more recent students that drivers late at night or students looking out their dorm room windows would see James walking back and forth between the Cross and Gorgas, usually on one of the rises along that road. He has also been seen in rooms and in the halls of both Gorgas and Quintard.

Ghost Man and Dog

Sometime in 2003, when they were living in central campus, George and Randy decided to take a late-night walk down Tennessee Ave. toward the Cross. When they started to approach the Cross, George noticed a small dog trotting along next to Randy. Since it looked friendly enough, he reached over to pat it on the head. His hand slipped right through where the neck would have been! Needless to say, George was shocked; he stopped in his tracks and looked at Randy, who had gone white as a sheet. When George looked back to confirm what he had seen, the dog was gone.

"Dude," said George, "did you see that dog?"

"No," replied Randy. "I was looking at the guy who was just standing behind you." Both of them walked back in silence.

Author's Note

This is the only "ghost dog" story told to me, but there are a few older ones still circulating around campus, and "ghost dogs" have apparently been a fairly common occurrence in the Domain over the years. I have to wonder, though, who the ghostly man would have been in this particular case...perhaps an owner reunited with his old companion?

The story is a little reminiscent of the story of Dr. Dabney, the first professor to die in Sewanee. He lived in one of the houses along Tennessee Avenue. After his death students meandering to Proctor's Hall, one of the many overlooks on campus and one popular with proctors in the past, at night (this was before the Cross was built) would feel someone put his arm around them as if escorting them along their way. Then, after a small walk, he slipped away and left them alone. He was never, however, reported to travel with a dog. Dr. Dabney, when he died at age 46, was the oldest person at that time to be buried in the University Cemetery.

The Headlights at the Cross

I received two very similar versions of this story: one from someone who knew the person involved and one from a person who actually experienced it. One occurrence was in 1950 and the other was later.

In those days, the cross was a favorite place to "neck". This particular night was during a dance weekend (now called party weekend). In those days Sewanee was all male and many of the students "imported" dates for the special weekends. Trudy came to see her boyfriend and had a double date with some friends. They headed down to the fraternity house and danced a few numbers.

The weather was finally dissolving into spring. The fog had left and the night was actually a little warm for a change — warm enough for Trudy and friends to open the cover on the car. What a gorgeous night, they decided, for a visit to the Cross.

With Trudy's boyfriend, Harry, at the wheel, they set off, all in a rather jovial mood, heading to the cross for the view of the valley and perhaps to enjoy some snuggling. Between Proctor's Hall Road and the cross there were no side roads or residences. The *only* road was the straight graveled road between the academy campus and the cross. This road was both noisy and often dusty, and it had three dips.

Trudy, Harry, and the rest had pulled off the road just to the Sewanee side of the cross to park a little while. Before long they saw it: a pair of headlights appeared beginning just about at the academy. The headlights went down into the first dip, came up over that rise and went down into the second dip, came up over that rise and went down into the third dip and never came up. Then it started again. After seeing this a few times they were struck with amazement. They decided to get out of there and Harry started the car. As they pulled into the road the bright lights of an older vintage of automobile appeared right in front of them. Understandably Harry jerked the car to the right and into a shallow ditch to avoid a head-on collision, but no car passed

119

them! There were no tire noises on the gravel road. There was no motor noise. The "car" had simply disappeared.

The ghost of the headlights at the cross is reported to be the spirit of a Sewanee resident who was killed in an automobile accident going down the mountain to Chattanooga in 1935 or 1936. One of his favorite pastimes was to drive to the Cross to watch the sunset and see the flickering lights come on in the towns below. Various versions of this story have popped up over the years. Most of the time students see the headlights but not the car close up.

The Man on the Track

A long-time resident of Sewanee has seen a ghost at the University track on two separate occasions. This track circles the University's football field, which is flanked by Texas Avenue, Florida Avenue, and Curlique Road. In the early days of the University the field was a baseball field for the popular Hardees team. When football got started the team practiced on the field, then called Hardee field. It has been used as the official football field since the University's first game in 1891. It is currently called McGee Field. The track serves as a social area for football games, but has also seen its share of track and field events.

This resident used to live near the outdoor track, and liked to go walking around it when she had a chance, which was usually late at night. One night she was walking counter-clockwise around when she saw in the distance another person walking in the opposite direction. She really didn't think much of it. Sewanee is a small town and generally safe, and people think nothing of walking alone late at night.

As they got closer to each other, she noticed that he appeared to be dressed in an old-fashioned suit, maybe from the forties or fifties, and he wore a bowler hat. As they passed each other, he tipped his hat at her and smiled. It was only after she passed that it registered with her that he just seemed odd and out of place. She turned around to get another look, but he had vanished.

Although it all seemed strange, she did not think that much about it, until it happened again one night. She realized that no one dressed the way he did any more, and he disappeared much too suddenly to have simply walked away. After that she walked earlier in the evening.

Perhaps some of you are brave enough to get out there late at night and see what you can see, and perhaps even identify him.

University Cemetery

In 1988 Veronica was walking from Woods Lab into the cemetery towards Wiggins Hall (which was a music building in this student's day but which is now the firefighters' dorm). She suddenly felt a cold chill unlike any she had ever felt before. It was to the bone – not scary but distinctly different and *other*. As she remembers it, there was no wind or cold temperature to explain the feeling.

The cemetery was always a comforting place to walk. She never minded cutting through there even in the dark. She can't explain what she felt, but still remembers the feeling quite clearly. It was the first time she really wondered if there were ghosts.

This is the cemetery that holds Francesca. See the story for McCrady Hall to learn about Francesca. And remember, upon leaving a cemetery you should tell the ghosts firmly not to follow you.

Several years ago, when walking back from the Pub past the cemetery Daphne saw a lady in an old white dress who turned around and gave her "a look." She was walking past one cemetery entrance to the next one, ostensibly looking for her husband, who was moved to another cemetery.

Commercial Spots

DuBose Conference Center

The land that DuBose Conference Center is on was originally donated for a women's college called Fairmount. Dr. DuBose was married to one of the women who owned the school, and he served in some capacity at the school. After the school closed, William Sterling Claiborne used the site for a Training School for Episcopal priests, and those students served many of the 28 missions of Otey parish in Sewanee. The old school burned and the white Spanish style building replaced it. The Conference Center has been operating for many years.

I (the author) feel compelled to mention DuBose because it was the very first place on the Mountain about which I ever heard a ghost story. I went to Camp Gailor-Maxon at DuBose Conference Center for a number of years when I was young. The very first day of my first year (and every year afterwards) the counselors pointed out to us the haunted fourth floor of the center. There were only a few rooms on the fourth floor, and they were never used for campers. Their story was that Dr. DuBose, after whom the center was named, was a mean, evil old man – so mean that someone pushed him to his death from the fourth floor balcony. There was a portrait of Dr. Dubose hanging in the main lobby, and he certainly looked like a stern old man. The fable was a very effective way to keep us campers off the fourth floor. I didn't learn until years later that Dubose was actually quite beloved and that nothing of the sort had happened to him.

The story of Dr. DuBose was embellished over the years and it evolved into several different ones. One night David Ellingham, one of that year's camp counselors, decided to scare the dickens out of the campers. After they were settled into their cabins for the night, he dressed in a cape and hood and went walking in the fields near the cabins, holding a lantern in front of him. He floated silently across the field waiting for the screaming to begin. Suddenly, he heard the cocking of a shotgun behind him. Whipping around and throwing up his hands, knowing he was about to meet his end, he came face to face with Winnie Walker, the manager of the conference center. "DON'T SHOOT! It's just me, David," he yelled. After a pregnant pause, Winnie lowered her shotgun. "David Ellingham, I thought you were an intruder. Why didn't you warn me what you were doing? I could have shot you!" The joke was on David that night!

That was the last time Dr. DuBose appeared in that field.

While we did have fun scaring the campers with Dr. DuBose stories, we did not relate the real ghost story of DuBose Conference Center, one that has remained consistent with each telling. It is a story that has been corroborated over the years by people with no connection with each other:

Elana was sleeping in one of the double rooms. A fog began to drift in underneath the closed door. It slowly formed itself into a vaguely human form, the form of a girl. The fog seemed somehow dense and tangible. The fog figure sat down in the rocking chair and began to rock and rock and rock until all the fog disappeared, but the chair kept rocking.

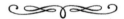

Another room on the second floor is also haunted, the last room on the East wing. A girl named Sidney is said to have hanged herself in the closet. She haunts the room to this day. Many who stay in the room have said they have felt her presence.

Julia's father used to be the Executive Director at DuBose. Whenever she stayed with her parents, she would go to his office in the main building to check her email. Invariably she would hear footsteps and doors opening and closing, even though she was the only person in the building and all the doors were locked. It was always spooky going into that building by herself.

Edgeworth Inn

Stephanie had come up to help her son move out of his dorm, and the only place she could find to stay was the Edgeworth Inn, a bed and breakfast place in the Monteagle Assembly grounds. They gave her a very nice room behind the kitchen.

She was there by herself, and there were terrible thunderstorms all night. Lightning flickered constantly, casting dancing shadows across the room, and the wind whistled rudely in the otherwise quiet spot. Stephanie settled into an uneasy sleep.

In the middle of the night Stephanie was jolted awake by a bright light in the room. It wasn't lightning; the television had come on. Startled, she lay a while, allowing the hiss of the TV to fill the room. Finally she got up and turned it off, and got back into bed. She must have dropped off to sleep again, because she was aroused once again as the television came on again. Stephanie had to unplug it. Soon thereafter, the alarm clock began to ring, though it was set for a different time.

Eventually Stephanie slept. By morning she had convinced herself that the storm had caused the electrical anomalies in the room.

When she went to breakfast, the owners asked how she had slept. She said she had barely slept all night because of all the activity. Instead of agreeing that everything was storm related, they brushed it off and mentioned casually that they thought the room was spooked. Stephanie most certainly agrees!

Julia's

A little girl in a white nightgown wanders around outside the former Julia's Restaurant. Have you seen her?

Mi Casa Restaurant

The staff who work at Mi Casa, the Mexican restaurant halfway between Sewanee and Monteagle, see a ghostly figure quite often, especially when cleaning up late at night after the restaurant is closed. The ghost especially likes to hang out around the little spiral staircase that goes to the attic, or around the kitchen window. They are kind of used to him, but all the same take care not to annoy him.

Mont Milner Camp Area

Blake was driving home late one night. His family lives off of Gudger Road, about eight miles from campus. The turn onto Gudger Road is just past a lake with a camp on it called Mont Milner. There is not usually much activity out there, and never at night. This night as Blake was passing by, he saw a figure dressed in what looked like a nun's outfit standing outside holding a lantern and glowing. He could not believe it! After staring for a minute, he raced home to get his camera. When he got back, however, the place was as dark as it always is. What did he see?

Monteagle Inn

Mia had an experience with her husband at what is now the Monteagle Inn. They spent the Sunday night after their wedding at the Inn. All of their other guests had left and the staff of the Inn had gone home. They were alone in the Inn, getting their things together for the next day, when they heard a sound like footsteps squeaking on the main staircase. They both froze, and Mia's husband poked his head around the corner to look and say, "Is anyone there?" There was no answer, and there was definitely no one in the Inn.

St. Mary's

St. Mary's is an Episcopal Convent that was also a school until 1968. Quite a few buildings have been associated with St. Mary's since its beginning. The ghost stories associated with St. Mary's involve buildings that were part of the school at one time and also a house that used to be on the St. Mary's Road.

A red brick building on the campus used to be the Convent and one of the school buildings. In recent years it has been used for retreats, conferences, and weddings. It is located on a beautiful spot on the brow of the mountain offering a gorgeous view of sunsets. Apparently some spirits really enjoy the location as well.

Some visitors have asked about the nun who still wears a habit, only to be told it is the spirit of a former nun. Many believe her to be the charming Sister Hughetta, a very devoted nun and the woman responsible for bringing the Order to the mountain. Sister Hughetta was a member of the prominent Snowden family of Memphis. She was a novice in 1878 when a horrible yellow fever epidemic ravaged the city. The nuns in Memphis did all they could to help the sick and dying. Most of them died during the epidemic, but Sister Hughetta managed to survive. Around the turn of the century, Bishop Quintard, bishop of the Episcopal Church of Tennessee, convinced her to come to Sewanee to open a school for mountain girls. There is still a group of nuns who live at St. Mary's. Sister Hughetta sometimes appears to children and pulls pranks like turning lights on and off or making the sound of her footsteps.

A priest was preaching in the chapel at St. Mary's one Sunday when he witnessed a spirit come into the chapel and sit down, looking at him intently. The message he received from the spirit was to clean up his act! He did!

Another man has seen a group of children playing Ring Around the Rosy on the grounds of St. Mary's.

Near the old convent was a house that at one time was home to a family with seven children. One night a huge storm was raging outside. The wind whistled through every crack and thunder shook the small frame farm cottage. All of a sudden the lights flickered. At that moment one of the daughters was heading to the kitchen. She looked into the living room to see a terrifying scene. An entire family in nineteenth century clothing was huddled together, and the father was guarding the door with an ax. Someone was outside trying to get in and she had the horrible feeling that the family was murdered by whoever was out there. Then the lights flickered again and the scene vanished. She saw that vision several other times.

One day Sadie, one of the daughters, wanted to go to town. The family car was not working. Her father called TL, a neighbor, to give Sadie a ride. Sadie did not want to go with TL. He made unwelcome advances to her. She did not know how to tell her father this. Luckily, another neighbor offered to give her a ride. She knew that TL would probably be angry. TL, however, did not have a chance to be angry. As he was heading to their house, he passed by the Cloisters, a private home that used to be a dorm for the St. Mary's school. At that moment he heard a loud voice tell him, "Someone else is giving Sadie a ride to town." No one was in sight that could have said that. Rattled, TL went to the family home to tell them what he had heard. To this day they all wonder who the voice could have been.

The Cloisters has a ghost of its own. Could the voice have been that of the resident ghost? One woman who cleaned there at one time left the job because she kept feeling someone touch her on the shoulder. Invariably, when she turned around no one was ever there.

Another person reported that there used to be a portrait in the stairwell. The figure in the portrait was blue. One night, however, when he descended the stairs, the portrait had turned blood red.

Still others say that the spirit of a young girl resides there. She was a student at the school when it was a school for mountain girls. Besides reading and writing, the school taught such practical subjects as housekeeping, sewing, and gardening. One year there was a scarlet fever epidemic. The little girl died, but her spirit remained. She has the reputation of being a matchmaker and spreader of good cheer. Did she inform TL that Sadie found another ride to town? It took care of Sadie's problem. TL never bothered her again.

Shenanigans

There are two ghosts downstairs at Shenanigans that seem to hang around, mostly when a staff member is working alone. One is a gray and black figure, and the other wears a white shirt. Mr. Winn, who ran Winn's grocery there for many years, may be one of them. He likes to make noises and slam doors and things. You can hear his pocket watch.

Not long before the restaurant changed hands the ghosts began to appear more frequently. It was hard to tell if they were unhappy or simply watching over the place as usual. Usually they appeared only during the foggy season of the year, but that year they continued their presence into the summer. They appeared to be quietly observing, not making their usual noises.

Shenanigans had a facelift during the 2009-2010 school year. For years it was leaning and looked as if it might fall down one day. Now it is straight again and stands tall and blue with its red tin roof and trim. The front door does not drag, and the hole in the wood floor at the entrance is fixed. New windows adorn the front. It has, however, retained its cozy old building feel.

The restaurant has had two sets of new owners since the ghosts made the above-mentioned appearances. Have the newest owners noticed the ghosts?

Residences

Bob Stewman Road

Shirley was in the kitchen of her house on Bob Stewman Road. Suddenly she heard cello music. She was a cellist, but she certainly wasn't playing the cello at that time. She went into the living room and there was her cello playing itself!

Brinkwood

    Callie's grandparents owned Brinkwood, a lovely estate located on Natural Bridge Road. Her grandfather had been a captain in the Air Force, so everyone called him Captain Wilson. During his retirement days in Sewanee he helped run Sewanee's small airport and he raised lots of money for Sewanee. He and his wife, like many others who have moved to the Mountain, became loyal supporters of the University.

    Brinkwood has one of the most beautiful views in the whole area, opening up into Lost Cove where you could literally be above the clouds some days. The fogs and mists would often sink into the cove. No houses or roads marred the view. Most of the cove is now in an environmental land trust, so it will remain wild and undeveloped for generations to come. This property had the added benefit of adjoining the Natural Bridge, a popular scenic stop for tourists and townspeople alike.

    It is unknown when the name first became attached to it. The estate was built in the early 1900's, and was once owned by author Walker Percy. There are now several houses on the land even though the property has a single owner. Callie's grandparents have long since left this world, although the grandfather has been seen now and again, surveying changes being made on the property. According to one construction worker, he apparently approves of what they are doing, because once he felt a pat on his back that clearly meant, "Good job, son," just the way Captain Wilson did it when he was alive.

The Castle

The house on Natural Bridge Road that is called "The Castle" had another name when it was built in the 1910's: "The Cliffs." The first owners, a New Orleans based family named Warriner, wrote about building this huge stone structure in just six weeks, even devising a rail system to haul stone to the property. In the 1960's Mrs. Clara Shoemate ran a restaurant there, and called it Claramont Castle. It was also used as a hotel of sorts for a while. Now it is simply called The Castle. Owned by members of the Henley family, it currently stands vacant, although the nearby caretaker's cottage has an occupant.

In 1969, Dr. Figaro, a new Art professor, moved into the Castle with his young family. Before they moved in the house had been shut up for about a year. Dr. Figaro opened the windows to let some fresh air in and the dampness out.   The first night he slept on the dusty, mold-smelling floor in the downstairs lobby, with a mother cat and kittens the family had brought with them. During the night he was awakened by crashing as the window screens, one after the other, fell from the many upstairs windows. These screens kept falling out of the window frames on and off during the night regardless of the side of the house or wind pattern. He wondered if the house was haunted.

From the beginning the house seemed to be inhabited by something other than the family. The family often had the uncanny feeling that someone was in the next room or elsewhere in the house. Dr. Figaro would check to see if someone had come into the house to visit, but no one was ever there. Once, when walking into the living room from the kitchen, he saw a group of people having a party. Their clothes and hair dated to early in the twentieth century. Momentarily, this "image" disappeared as in the manner of a mirage.

The family frequently walked from the house to the Sherwood Road and back, on Natural Bridge Road, or down to the pond. On these occasions they turned off the house lights, but on many, many of these occasions they returned to find lights on throughout the house.

Every night before going to bed, Dr. Figaro checked every single room in the house. He checked the cellar, which was spooky with or without ghosts, and the attic stairwell, and he climbed to the tower room and looked into the attic off the landing. This attic seemed to have two large spaces. One was visible by opening the door and the other was around the tower and not visible. He always feared he'd find a dead body in the back area of the attic so did not ever go there.

After living in the Castle for three years, Dr. Figaro decided to tackle the difficult task of entering into the part of the attic in which none of them had ever set foot. When he did, he saw an older man in a brown suit sitting in a corner on a chair. Surprised and unnerved, Dr. Figaro spoke to him telepathically, projecting his thoughts that he would have to leave the Castle because they were a young family that now lived there and would for a while. The old man said nothing in response to his projection. Dr. Figaro then said aloud various prayers and made the sign of the cross. He was trembling. Then he high-tailed it out of the attic tower room, and down the steep stairs to the second floor where two guests were playing with his sons and his wife was preparing their daughter for bed. He later related his experience to his wife.

One morning their son woke up early and began to play in the hall. Then he saw a figure floating down the hallway toward him. He rushed into his parents' bedroom and crawled under the covers between them.

Eventually the family bought a house of their own and moved out. It was not, however, the end of the story. One evening, just before Christmas, Dr. Figaro offered to drive a man to his home. He recognized that the man had been caretaker of the Castle and lived in a small wooden house next door on the same property.

On the drive out the Sherwood Road the man asked, "Didn't you live at the Castle once?" When Dr. Figaro replied in the affirmative, the man asked if he ever noticed anything unusual while living there, to which Dr. Figaro replied, "Do you mean a ghost?" The man became excited because for a long time he had wanted to relay his own story about experiencing the ghost of the Castle. He had always feared folks would think his images were merely hallucinations from drinking.

The caretaker related that once, when he was preparing to retire for the night, he stepped onto his porch for some fresh air. He noticed all of the lights on in the Castle, yet no one lived in the building at that time. With gun in hand, he unlocked the door and walked up the stairs to the hallway. He was shocked to see an old man drifting toward him from the far end of the hall. He was so startled he shot once or twice at the apparition, which promptly disappeared.

One day after classes Dr. Figaro went to the campus pub with some of the students, and they began sharing ghost stories. When Dr. Figaro related his own experience from the Castle, one of the students said his great-grandfather from New Orleans had had the Castle constructed, and that a book had been printed about its construction and he would have his mother send a copy for him. Dr. Figaro was teaching when the book arrived. At the end of the afternoon when he returned home, his wife showed him various photographs, page after page, covering any information with her hand. Dr. Figaro did not understand why she was doing this but complied, and soon realized her intention when she turned to a photograph of the man who had built and owned the house on the cliff. It was the very same man he had seen as a ghost in the attic.

Note: The book, titled *The Way it Was*, by Alfred Louis Warriner, is available in the University of the South library.

The Cave

There is a house on South Carolina Avenue that was built by the Bratton family in 1938. The most recent owner served as alumni director for many years, and has always remained close to students and alumni he knows. He rents several rooms to students each year, and one is in his basement. The room is dark and cool like a cave, and also a little creepy at times.

Dillon lived in the Cave one summer. On one particularly average night, he had gotten in bed when he noticed some sort of phantom that was hovering about three or four feet above him. He could make out a distinct, humanoid form but other than that the figure was entirely featureless. At first he thought his eyes were playing tricks on him, but the phantom remained in his position swaying gently left and right, for a solid two or three minutes before he or she disappeared. This happened on two separate occasions; a few weeks later the same phantom emerged again and visited Dillon for a few minutes, confirming his suspicion that the phantom was of supernatural origin.

Curlique Road House

Wanda and Lawrence Cheston built this house in the 1990's on the old Sara Dudney lease. Sara's house had burned during the ice storm of 1985. Bad karma appeared to plague that site. Mr. John Hodges, Sara's neighbor and friend, had had a heart attack and died in her kitchen.

Wanda always felt bad vibes in that house and so did her children. One night the kids had a friend spend the night. The next morning the little girl said, "Your grandmother came in last night to tell us to go to bed." Wanda's girls looked at each other. They did not have a grandmother living with them.

Deepwoods

The name for the community of Deepwoods is quite appropriate. A road leads three miles from the main highway to the bluff and it just gets deeper and deeper into the woods. There are areas that feel quite secluded, and Shirley's house is no exception. There is absolutely no traffic out where she lives.

Shirley had multiple incidents occur in her home in Deepwoods. She tried to rid the house of the presence with sage, holy water, and even with some spiritual Indian feathers sent to her from Oregon along with the appropriate accompanying rituals.

The same week that Shirley moved to Deepwoods, her neighbor across the way, Dr. David, was hacked to death by his own chain saw not far from the road. She didn't hear anything but something made her walk outside on the porch to look around and listen. She didn't know he had crawled to the end of the drive and lay there bleeding to death.

She cried for two weeks because she felt she had not paid enough attention. Since the grisly death she has had vases break in half, doors swing open, trails of brown goop on the walls throughout the house, and much, much more. She has become rapidly disabled as if the life is being sucked out of her.

People have commented for years that the house has a sense of heaviness or oppression about it. Is Dr. David causing the heaviness?

deRosset House

This house, a large, square house on Tennessee Avenue, was built in 1872 by a man named John Elam, but is known by the name of the couple who lived there the longest, Armand and Rachel deRosset. They both lived well into their nineties. Mr. deRosset did not like dogs, and once made the provost come over and listen for several hours to a tape recording of a dog who had been barking the night before.

Keri lived in the deRosset house. The house was split into two sides with both sides having kitchens. She and her roommate lived on the right side and had a definite dweller. The ghost was often heard climbing the stairs. One night during Family Weekend Keri had her parents' golden retriever in the house. He started barking like crazy and running around and then they heard the downstairs door slam and someone climbing the stairs. Keri got up and confirmed the noise with her roommate and they both went downstairs together and confirmed that the door was still locked so no one had come in. They continued to hear that on many occasions. At other times they saw lights flashing in and out of their drawers.

They ended up having a house blessing performed by Keri's roommate's father who is an Episcopal priest. They did not have trouble after that.

Elliott Cottage

This cute cottage, recently enlarged, was built for Mrs. Stephen Elliott in 1870 to house students. Her own house still stands next door. The cottage is still owned by members of the Elliott family. The owner relates this story:

"A guest in our home at 56 Tennessee Ave (Elliott cottage) described a ghost at the top of our stairs. It was a small elderly woman concerned with our guest's comfort, a very welcoming presence. We decided it was my Aunt Isabelle Howe, because she was definitely a good hostess.

"We reported this to my cousin Sarah (Isabelle's daughter) and she said she had just had a visit from her mother as well: Isabelle's chime clock that hadn't worked in years started chiming when all Sarah's family was gathered for a dinner. That was up in Maryland, not in Sewanee. But we thought it confirmed our guess as to the identification of our ghost.

"I like thinking that Aunt Isabelle is still in the house."

Garnertown Road Area

Willow lived with her boyfriend, Juan, in the area of town called Garnertown. She was a student at the University, and it was midterms. Willow went to Mi Casa restaurant to study and have dinner while waiting for Juan to finish up there (because he worked there). She was so tired from writing papers and studying that she went home early before Juan got off work. She crawled into bed and went to sleep.

Willow woke up suddenly about twenty minutes later because she felt someone watching her. She turned around and as her eyes adjusted to the dark she could see a man wearing a plaid shirt standing by the bed. She couldn't see his face because it was so dark. She instinctively reached out to touch him, thinking it was Juan, and stuck her hand right through him.

As soon as she did that, the figure started to disappear. Willow was shocked, but the thought that went through her head was "Oh my god, I just saw a ghost, but it didn't feel like a scary ghost. It just felt like it was watching over me." She went back to sleep.

When Juan got home she woke up again and told him, "Maybe I'm just going crazy because I could have sworn I saw a ghost tonight!" He told her that he, his brother, and one of his employees had seen one that night at around eleven in Mi Casa, the Mexican restaurant halfway between Sewanee and Monteagle, the same time she saw the man in the plaid shirt.

Just to add more evidence that it really happened, Juan's brother and his employee both told Willow the same story the next day before they got to talk to Juan! They all told her that they were talking near the spiral staircase in the restaurant when they all saw a figure that was like "smoke or ashes or dust" that was in the shape of a human drifting past the entrance to the kitchen. Could the two encounters have been the same ghost? Why did they see them at the same time?

Back to the house on Garnertown Road – when Juan first moved in, there were lots of stuffed animals there. He woke up one night to find one had been tossed into his face, and his brother woke at the same time to find the same thing. The former owners said the ghost of a little boy lived there, and the man in the plaid shirt was the grandfather. The grandfather had paid them visits on numerous occasions.

HerJim Road

There is a house around the corner from Juan and Willow's on a road named HerJim Road. A visitor to this home saw Elvin King dressed in his burial clothes while everyone else was out at his funeral.

Judd House

The last time this house was for sale, the two real estate agents showing the house had quite a story to tell about one of their showings. A man came to look at the house, and the two agents showed him through the inside as usual. Then they went outside to show off the ample back yard. When they came back into the kitchen, a lighted candle was sitting on the counter. That prospective buyer certainly lost interest in the house, and the current owners have had no trouble whatsoever.

The former owner always said that the ghost was Spencer Judd, the former University photographer, who lived in the house for many years until he died. A lighted candle was his signature for being around when he was not happy. He did not like the husband of the family who lived there, and reportedly appeared to him after lighting a candle and made him fear for his life! To the man's wife, however, he was comforting and benevolent, keeping her company during the husband's long absences and holding long conversations with her.

To the community, Spencer Judd was an avid outdoorsman and a marvelous photographer who located his business in Sewanee from the 1870's until his death. Most of the University's early best quality photos were his work. Most memorable are his views of Proctor's Hall, Morgan's Steep, Natural Bridge, the village, and the old railroad. When looking at his pictures you can't help but ask yourself where he was possibly able to find a spot to stand with all of his equipment somewhere on a cliff where he would make 3x4 or 5x7 glass negatives. Legend has it that his wife threw his existing glass negatives down their well after he died, but quite a few of them survive to this day. Apparently his spirit remains, too, for noble purposes.

Kirby-Smith Clark Hurst House

This stately antebellum-style house of red brick with white columns sits at the head of Rowark's Cove Road and Texas Avenue directly across the street from the football field. Reynold Marvin Kirby-Smith, son of General Edmund and Maude Kirby-Smith, built this house in 1916. The current owners have done extensive renovations to the house. According to the workmen doing the renovations, the original owner lingers about. He has spooked them several times, especially out in the yard. He takes the form of a man dressed in white. He apparently approves of the progress.

One day one of the workmen was on a ladder outside the house. A movement in the bushes caught his eye. When he looked around, he saw a man dressed in white standing there observing him. It startled him, but he did not think too much about it. Anyone happening by might show the same curiosity. But something was not right. He did not seem to be completely there but was more like the shadow of a person dressed in clothing more suited to earlier times. Then he simply disappeared. When the other workers declared they had seen a ghost amid the bushes, it made his skin prickle. He knew they were right. He didn't believe in ghosts, but he saw this apparition often enough to change his thinking about that. The workers believe that it is Dr. Kirby-Smith watching the progress of the renovations.

Midway Road House

There is a house in Midway that was the scene of a tragic accident. It was just an ordinary day and Sherri was busily cooking in her kitchen. She picked up a knife and suddenly it slipped out of her hands and cut a major artery. Sherri bled to death before anyone could help her.

Now the current owner often sees the rocking chair moving. The lights constantly come on in the kitchen. She tied empty tobacco sacks over the door to keep the ghost away. Someone staying in her house heard someone walking down the steps and refused to stay there alone again.

Mikell Lane Rental House

The second house on the left when you turn onto Mikell Lane from Tennessee Avenue is a University rental traditionally inhabited by seminarians. One family who lived there in the 1990's reported that they had an amiable ghost who liked to rock in their outdoor rocker. Somehow it was decided that it must be the ghost of Dr. Torian, a pediatrician who retired to Sewanee and proceeded to practice for another twenty years, until he was 95. He liked to visit his patients at home, and perhaps he still does make his rounds.

Morgan's Steep Rental House

There is a house on the way to Morgan's Steep near the old hospital that isn't as quiet as it looks from the outside. This house has been rented to seminarians for decades. In the 1970's, Danielle babysat for the couple who lived there. They had a young baby. After putting him to bed one night, Danielle heard him crying. She went in to comfort him only to find him sound asleep. When she got out to the living room, the crying started again. She went back again, and he was still sleeping. Feeling a bit disturbed by this, she mentioned it to the couple when they came home. The mother exclaimed, "You hear it, too!" as if to say, "Thank God I'm not crazy!"

A couple of years ago I (the author) was helping with a Homecoming party at the new Archives house. It was a reunion of Kappa Sigmas. I was just starting to collect ghost stories at the time. The subject of ghosts came up with one of the alums, and he said, "The only story I know about is the crying baby at the house on Morgan's Steep Road." I was stunned. Two identical stories from unrelated sources, again! I had just gotten two corroborating stories about McCrady dorm the week before. I believe that's what made me decide to continue collecting these stories.

Reynolds House

Colonel Reynolds still lingers at home
Round the house and the yard he will roam
Giving workmen the creeps
Scaring them into leaps
When he pops in and out like a gnome.

There is a house on Florida Avenue that is visited by the
ghost of the man who used to live there: George Reynolds,
Senior. Colonel Reynolds came to Sewanee to work at the
Sewanee Military Academy. The first house he rented, the
Sanborn house, was haunted, too. A picture in the possession of
the current owner confirms that Colonel Reynolds is the spirit
hanging around the house on Florida Avenue. The new owners of
the house are part-time Sewanee residents. When they first
purchased the house, they had the house renovated. Their
workman practically lived over there while completing
renovations on the older home. Many times he saw this ghost
checking out his work. The ghost never approached him. He
merely watched. The workman was able to identify Colonel
Reynolds by the picture. He is not a mean ghost. He is simply

curious about what is happening to his former home. Still, it was quite unnerving to have Colonel Reynolds suddenly pop in and then just as suddenly vanish.

Rivendell

A Sewanee alum named this estate on Natural Bridge Road. He owned it during the 1980's and 1990's. The original owners, the Mitchells, had a summer camp, Camp Thorwald, more affectionately known as Camp Whoopie, on the several acres tucked away among old growth trees. The property still has remnants of an old swimming pool on the grounds. There are two houses left; one a big laid-stone mansion and the other a small stone back house. The small back house serves as a rental home. The big house for the most part stood empty for a number of years and is now used for meetings of a writers' group. The secluded grounds can be a bit spooky at night or even during the day.

Janet lives in the little house behind the big one. One morning she was awakened by something tugging at her toes. When she opened her eyes, a little girl with blonde hair in a blue dress was standing there. "Where is my mother?" she asked. Janet, startled, sat up in bed. At that point the little girl disappeared. Since then, she has seen the girl many times, usually in her bedroom, and always inquiring about her mother. Once in the living room of the big house the little girl appeared and pointed to the portrait of a woman over the fireplace. "Where is my mother?" she is asking. Occasionally a little boy appears. He also tugs at Janet's feet.

Janet told her story to me (the author) because she knew I was collecting ghost stories. I was excited to get it. When I got home my daughter, Sarah, and her friend Hope were there. "I got a new story today," I said. "It's about Rivendell."

"Oh," Hope said, "is it the little girl with blonde hair in the blue dress?" My mouth fell open. "Yes," I replied. "How did you know that?"

"A friend of mine used to rent that little back house at Rivendell. The little girl used to come tug on her toes and ask where her mother was."

I took that as corroborating evidence. If you're ever walking on those grounds, look around for the little girl in the blue dress and the little boy. Maybe you can help them.

Sanborn Cravens Home

The Sanborn/Cravens family has had a long association with the University and has been a presence on the Mountain for a hundred years or more. Marymor Sanborn, from New Orleans, ran one of the boarding houses for summer visitors. The Cravens family was associated with the Sewanee Military Academy (Cravens Hall is named in honor of the family) and with the University Supply Store. The Sewanee Military Academy, also known over the years as the Sewanee Grammar School and the Sewanee Academy, was a college preparatory boarding school. The campus buildings included some that have ghost stories associated with them, namely Gorgas, Quintard, and the Tennessee Williams Center (the old SMA gym). Those are now University buildings, and the former Academy is now a merged school on a separate campus called St. Andrew's-Sewanee. But that's more than you needed to know for this particular story.

More on the Sanborn House

The ambling, gambrel-style yellow house with green roof was built in the early 1900s. For decades the inviting structure stood on Texas Avenue at the head of Florida Avenue, until it burned in 2004. Its replacement home, "Driftwood Redux," is reminiscent of the delightful old house. Boo Cravens, Marymor's daughter, lives there. The old house saw its share of family, friends, visitors, renters, and students, more than most in Sewanee. According to some, however, the ghost of the house did not like it when anyone other than a family member lived there.

The Ghost of the Sanborn House

Author's Note: This story is adapted from an unpublished one told by Mrs. Louise Ware.

Next door to the Sanborn house across from the athletic field lived Pete Ware and his wife, Louise. Pete, by coincidence, had the largest collection of shaving mugs in the world, all displayed at his home. On their front porch was also a marvelous carousel horse.

When Mrs. Ware first came to Sewanee she became very interested and somewhat involved in a ghost, or ghosts, who plagued all the tenants who lived in Marymor Sanborn's house. When she arrived, the house was rented to a young bride and groom, Joe and Anne Scott. He was teaching in the English Department. This young couple had quite a time with the Sanborn ghost, which seemed particularly vexed at their staying in the house. His vengeance was taken out in thunderous noises such as the crashing of china. Each investigation showed no signs of disorder or evidence of anything wrong. Their next concern was, after their retiring for the evening, hearing the doors slam back and forth. They were bewildered and naturally scared, so they decided to have new locks and bolts put on the doors. But ghosts are never foiled, for the Scotts would securely lock their doors and retire, only to be awakened by the slamming and banging of doors. Often they rushed down to find the doors partly open. They talked freely to us and to other friends about this situation and they were obviously disturbed. Then there was a "hush-hush campaign" about the ghost when Joe Scott was offered a job in another place and he wanted to sub-let the house.

One evening Pete and Louise were having dinner with the Scotts when they were startled out of their chairs by the banging and breaking and slamming out in the kitchen. Joe left the room, obviously to investigate. When he returned no discussion of what had happened took place; only an uneasy exchange of looks between the two. Pete and Louise respected their wish not to talk about it, and, of course, said nothing. But they had heard the noises the Scotts had so often told them about before.

The Scotts left Sewanee and the house was rented to Colonel and Mrs. Reynolds, and their daughter, Betty. (Colonel Reynolds now haunts another house in town.) Their experiences with the Sanborn Ghost were the most spectacular of all. They had the noises and the trouble with the locked doors slamming and banging in the night, but they also saw him.

One afternoon Mrs. Reynolds was in the bath with the door open. Glancing up at the stairway facing the open bathroom, she beheld a sight that frightened her so much she was unable to call or to scream. As related by Mrs. Reynolds, she saw a headless man walking up the stairs. When finally she could move or was able to make a sound, she called Betty, breathlessly, told her what she had seen, and then telephoned Colonel Reynolds to come home at once. The three together went up the stairs, looked into every room, but found no one. There was a room upstairs that was used for storage and the door was always closed. Having found no one thus far, they decided to go into the storage room. When Colonel Reynolds tried the door, it failed to open although it was not locked. Finally, with great force he got the door open, only to have it slammed hard in his face as though a strong and great gust of wind had blown it to. Persistence and courage got him into the room, but it was still and quiet and not a person or a ghost could be seen. This is the first story of the ghost they told to friends.

They were upset and mystified and quite scared. But they did not move out of the house. They lived on there to have another spectacular experience. This one is not so frightening but rather a pretty experience. One afternoon while Mrs. Reynolds was in the pantry preparing tea, she was reaching for cups on a high shelf. She suddenly felt the presence of someone in the room. She slowly turned with her eyes lowered. On the floor, she saw feet clad in black slippers with buckles. Looking upward, she beheld

170

legs in silk stockings, then knee breeches made of pink satin. She said to herself: "This is the Ghost. I have always wondered what his face was like, and now I shall see."

But she never saw his face. He was very, very, extraordinarily tall, and as her glance crept up the long, tall, thin figure, he disappeared – vanished into the air! Maybe he was the same ghost who went up the stairs only dressed in the kind of clothes he should wear to tea – and probably he just didn't HAVE a face! By this time, Colonel Reynolds was anxious to make friends with the ghost, and he would leave cake and wine out for him at night on the living room table. Evidently, the ghost did not fancy cake or wine, for he never touched it. The Reynolds never knew whether they were disappointed or relieved when they found their refreshments untouched.

The Reynolds' moved away from Sewanee, and the next tenants were General and Mrs. Allin. General Allin was the Superintendent of the Sewanee Military Academy. He was rather a stern man, matter-of-fact, without much sense of humor. Mrs. Allin was a lovely, dignified, and proper lady. The ghost gave them only minor troubles like moving things out of place. They complained that he would never leave the books they were currently reading on the tables, and that many were the times they found their possessions strewn around and in unlikely places. They never saw him, but they spoke freely about their conviction that he was there.

The Sanborn ghost has never been known to bother anyone in that house when Marymor was in residence. Marymor either scorned the idea that there were ghosts in her house, or she just didn't want her ghastly, ghostly stories told.

Boo Cravens, Marymor's daughter, recently related that her mother actually encountered the ghost a couple of times herself but refused to talk about it.

Sherwood Road House

A little girl dressed all in white
Visits a Sherwood Road house day and night
She makes the bed fly
While you wonder why
She's trying to put up such a fight.

There is a house on the Sherwood Road that inconspicuously sits on a little hill nestled under a huge ancient oak tree across the street from the O'Dear Cemetery, just before St. Mary's Road. A portion of this house is a log cabin that was built in 1840. It is most likely the oldest house still standing in the wider Sewanee area. The house belonged to the Green family for several generations before changing hands.

The ceilings inside are quite low. A tall person would have to stoop to walk through the living room. There have been several ghost encounters both inside and outside the house.

Carole didn't actually see the ghost, but she did have an unusual experience one evening. She was sitting on the sofa in the living room one evening, reading a book. It was warm outside so she had the door to the front porch open. The roof of the porch dips way down and there are two front doors with a yellow bug light in between. The light was off. She noticed her tabby kitten inside the screen door jumping up towards a bright white flashing light outside above the screen door. It couldn't be a car's headlights on the road, for the house was hidden from view by the hill in front, and the trees, and the dip in the porch roof. There was, nevertheless, a bright light at the top of the door.

That's what the kitten was interested in. It was white, and brighter than the light of a firefly. The kitten kept jumping at it, trying to catch it. After about a minute, Carole's curiosity got the better of her. She got up and walked over to the door to investigate. Immediately the light vanished. She heard nothing outside. It hadn't been a reflection, or a flashlight, or headlights, yet it was real. She had watched it for a whole minute. The kitten sat looking at the top of the door for a few seconds, lost interest, and walked away.

If the kitten hadn't seen it Carole would have thought she had imagined it. She never figured out a logical explanation for that bright, flashing light, but after the rest of the family had so many encounters with a ghost there, she decided it was the work of the spirit.

Sarah was plagued by footsteps walking through the gravel drive behind her. More than once she heard the footsteps and turned around to find nobody there.

Her sister Ella had more alarming encounters. Ella's bedroom was upstairs in the attic over the living room. One night she woke up in the middle of the night. She saw a white figure standing about five feet in front of her. She could tell it was a little girl with long dark hair in a white nightgown. They looked at each other for several seconds. Then Ella reached over to turn on the light and the figure vanished. She seemed harmless, but Ella was still pretty shaken by the experience. The little girl appeared at the end of her bed on several occasions.

One night Ella had a friend over. After they went to bed, in the middle of the night, they woke to see the little girl standing in the room. She didn't look happy. All of a sudden, Ella's bed rose up off the floor about two feet and then dropped back to the floor. Screaming, the girls leapt out of bed and ran downstairs. Ella couldn't sleep up there for a while after that!

The family discovered a grave across the street in the cemetery. The headstone identified it as the grave of Mary Green, daughter and namesake of Mary Green who lived to be 104 years old. Little Mary Green's life was cut short by illness. That did not stop her from returning home now and then.

Recently a family member twice heard the footsteps behind him, turned around, and saw Mary in her long hair and white nightgown. The first time he was spooked and went inside as quickly as possible. The next week she appeared again in the drive behind her. He stood there for a minute looking at her. She looked sad. "Are you ok?" he asked. At that the spirit vanished. She has not been sighted since that time.

Soper Ghost

The family of Mary W. Shepherd Soper owned this house on Oklahoma Avenue from 1914 to the 1980's. This handsome house, now owned by alums, used to be called Topsy Turvy, for the two rock structures on the leasehold.

A favorite story about ghosts, and one in which a very clever ghost seems at work is the one that Mr. David Shepherd and his daughter told concerning a wedding veil that Mary Shepherd Soper borrowed to use in her wedding. Most of those who remember that wedding and the lovely veil she wore are no longer with us. The owner of the veil was a dear friend of Mary's who lived in Atlanta. The families agreed at the time of the wedding that the Sopers would keep the veil in Sewanee until the owner called for its return. Hence, after the wedding the Sopers placed the veil in their vault to await disposition at a later time.

Some months after the wedding Mary and her husband were in Atlanta and during a visit with the friend, the subject of the veil came up. Much to their astonishment, the owner thanked the Sopers for its return. It seems that one afternoon someone appeared at the door with a box containing the veil. They opened the box from time to time to inspect the veil or show it to others who wished to admire it. Perhaps seven to ten people were shown the veil. Finally, it was packed away in the attic where it resumed its old resting spot.

The Sopers, at this time, imagined that Mary's parents must have decided to return the veil and so dismissed the thought from their minds. Upon return to Sewanee, however, the Shepherds were astonished at the tale and all of them went to the vault, where indeed the veil was found just as it had been stored. When the veil was returned, finally, the earlier delivery was sought in the attic only to find that it had disappeared in as strange a manner as it had appeared in the first place. The mystery was never solved.

University Avenue House
A True Spooky Non-Ghost Story

This story took place at the house three doors down University Avenue from Elliott Hall. It is not a ghost story but a true occurrence involving a live person. It might be creepier than a ghost story. The name is not real.

It was just another regular night, and Katy had another babysitting opportunity. This was her first time with this particular child, but he was very easygoing and her job was fairly easy.

As she was playing with the child, she spotted a life-size clown doll standing in a corner of the room. She didn't have a particular fear of clowns, but she couldn't help but be a little nervous. Those blank eyes were just staring off into space. "He just happens to be facing us," she thought. The child took no notice and so she continued playing, trying not to show her concern over the doll.

Later Katy made dinner for the two of them. She still couldn't get the clown out of her head, nor could she forget those eyes. After dinner, they went back to playing but this time Katy was feeling even more anxious. She would occasionally glance at the clown doll, but it would always have the same blank stare.

Finally, it was time for her to get the child ready for bed. The staircase was located right next to the clown doll, and Katy knew that she would have to pass it on her way up. "It's just a doll, nothing more," she thought to herself. "Besides, if the kid isn't afraid of it then why should I be afraid?" As she passed the doll, she could have sworn that the eyes followed her and the child. "It's just a trick of the light."

She helped the child brush his teeth and get ready for bed. But when she opened the door to the child's room, there was the clown! It was standing next to the bed and it stared right at both of them.

Katy screamed and grabbed the child and ran downstairs and locked herself in the kitchen. In hysterics she called the police saying that someone had broken into the house. The police came, went upstairs, and led the clown out of the house.

The child was completely oblivious to what had happened. But now Katy becomes very anxious when she sees any clown of any size.

Woodlands

    The Woodlands area of Sewanee is very close to the brow of the Mountain on the "Decherd" side of town. Long ago there was a road up the Mountain from the community of Decherd that Union and Confederate soldiers (and stagecoaches and travelers) used. The portion of the road that remains is called Breakfield Road (or "Brakefield," depending on which map you use as a reference). The Woodlands area made a great camping spot for soldiers traveling through, and many Civil War artifacts have been found in that area. Rowark's Cove Road, also known as Alto Road, is now the main road down that side of the Mountain. It is narrow, steep, and twisty and runs right past the Woodlands area.

    Houses in the Woodlands area of Sewanee were built in the 1950's and 1960's mostly to accommodate families of seminary students. (Sewanee is an Episcopal school that includes a seminary among its graduate programs.) The Woodlands were at that time affectionately called "Fertile Acres." Also in that area were two sets of World War Two army barracks that served as staff and student housing until they were demolished in the 1980's. Even though those student apartments were always on the brink of condemnation because they were so dilapidated, students loved living there because they could get off the University's meal plan and could live more independently than in a dorm. I (the author) was offered one of the apartments one year, but the holes in the floors and the feeling that rats would peek out from under the sink at me made me more grateful to stay in a dorm room. Rock houses, duplexes, and quadruplexes sprang up around these barracks, providing a grassy area for community gatherings and a play park.

In one of those houses, the ghost of a genial old man resides. At first, only one of the residents could see him. He was rather pleasant to have around, and did not really bother anybody. She especially saw him in the hallway. She even walked through him once. After a while her husband could see him, too. He could be the same spirit who haunts a few other places in that area, but I think we will never know for sure. I don't exactly understand why I do not have scores of stories from this area, but maybe people are just not telling.

The Headless Gownsman

The Headless Gownsman

The Headless Gownsman is Sewanee's most famous ghost, even if he isn't real. (Don't tell him I said that!) Several versions of the Headless Gownsman story float around the internet, and the student newspaper and yearbook have both included stories of the celebrated ghost. At least two published works contain Headless Gownsman stories.

I am including here former historiographer Mrs. Elizabeth Chitty's version that she wrote in 1985 but never published (retold with permission from the family of Mrs. Chitty). It has been annotated in some places, and brief descriptions of other versions of the story have also been added. After her article I have reproduced the poem about the ghost from an old Sewanee yearbook.

The Headless Gownsman

By Elizabeth Nickinson Chitty

The most famous of Sewanee ghosts is the Headless Gownsman, although he has not been reported lately. A scholarly description of him appears in W. K. McNeil's *Ghost Stories from the American South*. McNeil tells us that headless ghosts are frequently thought of as moving on horseback, a legend which has an English background and which the *Legend of Sleepy Hollow* has made familiar, but no horse appears in the gownsman story. There was at one time a Sewanee ghost that rode a foaming black horse, according to the very first *Cap and Gown* annual in 1892, but his appearances must have ended years ago. While McNeil says that headless ghosts often "appear for a specific reason, perhaps as an omen of impending death or to avenge an injury," Sewanee's gownsman has only a benign history.

He was not the first of Sewanee ghosts. The Perambulating Professor, Dr. Robert Dabney, had that claim until his monument was transferred from the neighborhood of St. Luke's Hall to his grave in the University Cemetery. The Headless Gownsman has been the most persistent of Sewanee ghosts and certainly has the largest bibliography.

We can date his debut to his appearance to one of the matrons, Mrs. Emma Tucker (Note: at that time all the students stayed in boarding houses presided over by responsible head residents, most often widows of the Civil War. Mrs. Tucker was one such matron). She was going from Forensic Hall (the one and only social hall of the time, located where the sun dial stands in the Quadrangle) to her home at Palmetto Hall (about where the McClurg patio sits) to prepare refreshments after a dance. W. M. Patterson in *Purple Sewanee* tells the story: The mountain air was damp and the hour close to midnight, when she passed along between the old St. Augustine's Chapel and its separate belfry, and emerged into the path beyond, which cut across toward the stile leading to Palmetto, she saw someone ahead of her approaching steadily, upon the same path. Apparently it was a student gownsman for he wore a flowing black robe, and his arms seemed to be laden with books. Naturally she was prepared for the usual courteous salute expected from all the students, and while he was still approaching, she endeavored quite unsuccessfully to make out his identity. She saw his face plainly and yet she began to feel sure that she had never seen him before. Moreover, to her extreme alarm and astonishment, he seemed to make no effort to get out of the path himself as he advanced, so that she found herself compelled to step aside for him. Her terror was unbounded when, as she turned to gaze at him, he disappeared completely. Staggered by her experience, she made a circular detour and re-entered the path at a lower point. Immediately he appeared a second time and obstructed her advance so that she stepped aside again to let him pass;

183

whereupon he disappeared as suddenly as before. Breathless and unstrung she finally arrived at Palmetto and related her adventure, which has come down as one of Sewanee's most frequently related stories. She was not a timid or hysterical person but she never again came back from Forensic alone.

This version of the Gownsman story gave him a head, but novelist Maristan Chapman (the pen name of Mary and Stanley Chapman) said, also in *Purple Sewanee*, that he lost his head while a resident of Wyndcliff Hall, the current home of Dr. and Mrs. Potter, past the Academy grounds. A student was studying late and disturbing his roommates. They threw a pillow at his candle and "just at that moment—the student's head rolled off. Simply that. The unlucky youth had studied too hard and overweighted his brains with this dismal result. But that was not all. He might have picked his head up and replaced it without more ado had not the whirling thoughts within imparted a rotary motion that quickly carried it beyond his reach...the Head escaped downstairs—bumb-bump-bump" The Chapmans, who lived at Sewanee about 1930, maintained that the head could be heard still, rolling down the stairs of the house.

Seminary graduate Reese Hutcheson told Mr. McNeil that the ghost had moved to St. Luke's Hall, where it could be heard rolling down the stairs in his day in the 1970's, especially at exam times.

A similar version of the matron's encounter with the Headless Gownsman appeared in the 1956 student newspaper. That version attributes the sighting to Miss Johnnie Tucker, Mrs. Emma Tucker's daughter, and makes the gownsman headless. That version gives two alternate possibilities of how the ghost lost his head; a student who committed suicide or a student who fell from the dissecting room in Thompson Hall when it was a medical school building.

Arthur Ben Chitty, in his preface to The *Witch of Shakerag Hollow* by Marcia Hollis, places the origin of the ghost about 1880 and his habitat as Breslin Tower, which was built in the latter part of that decade. The tower was until the 1930's a hollow structure, with a long bell rope hanging from the clock level. Chitty claimed that the Gownsman, annoyed by the installation of steel and concrete floors in Breslin, moved to the tower of St. Luke's Chapel. He is also said to frequent Shapard Tower, where former carilloneer Albert Bonholzer was careful not to disturb the resident ghost (that tower, attached to All Saints' Chapel, holds a 56 bell carillon).

The Headless Gownsman was the subject of an 8mm documentary made in 1971 by the Bates brothers of Sewanee. Another tale attributes the gownsman's death to an accident in front of Wyndcliff Hall that decapitated a student.

The *Cap and Gown* of 1908 recounted in ballad style a more sinister version:

The Ballad of the Headless Gownsman, from the *Cap and Gown*, 1908, page 102:

> The hour was not of Thursday night
> Nor yet of Friday morn'
> But 'twas the time when night is dead,
> The morning still unborn.
>
> The moon discovered not a cloud
> Except the milky way.
> A somber, weird, and wizard light,
> Did make a semi-day.
>
> And long, lean shadows lay around
> From statuary trees,
> As masts of vessels, in the calm,
> Reflected on the seas.

And I was slowly walking on,
Affected by the gloom.
Augustine's Chapel, on my right,
Seemed truly "Gustine's tomb.

Dark, solemn, dull it looked—as it
Stood in the moonlight there.
I glanced at it unconsciously,
And then—I stopped to stare.

There was a man in front of it
A Gownsman, still as dead.
I looked at him—I looked again
My God! He had no head!

My feet stopped going—my blood stopped
flowing,
My muscles petrified.
I stood and stared—and never dared
To move to either side.

At last, full dazed, a foot I raised,
And feebly tried to go'
But all in vain—I must remain,
A voice, unheard, said "No."

Then with a stately, measured tread,
The Spirit moved to me;
Closer, closer came it, and
More clearly could I see.

It was a man without a head;
He wore a draping gown.
One hand was pointed straight at me,
The other pointed down.

And as he slowly drew to me,
I slowly drew to him,
Unable to resist I went
My sight began to dim.

The finger pointing to me said,
"On earth no longer dwell,
I need your life, I'll send you to"—
The downward hand said—"Hell."

We moved until a foot or so
Was 'tween his hand and me.
The finger, level with my face,
Was all my eyes could see.

And then I heard a hollow voice,
I saw no human face,
Yet words I heard and they were real,
They came from empty space.

In dreadful gones the Spectre spoke:
"I've waited long for you,
They took my head—I need one, and
I think that yours will do."

Two bony hands reached out at me
O God, they seized my head!
And I till now so still and stark,
All limp and loose—fell dead.

Came then a dream—I saw a stream,
Of boiling blood 'twas full.
I stood along, in a boat of bone,
'twas made of a monster skull.

The current rushed me onwards 'tween
The sun-lit, shining shores,
All full of ghastly, grinning heads
Piled high in countless scores.

I looked askance, in horror, at
The endless, awful scene.
I heard sweet, magic music notes,
With discords in between.

And then I woke—I lay all limp.
'twas just at breaking dawn.
I raised my hands and felt, and felt,
O God! My head was gone!

He had it, he had taken it,
That demon in the gown.
I cursed him—then I heard a laugh
In mockery resound.

I stayed, deep buried under earth,
For one entire week,
And in that time, I oft resolved
Another head to seek.

So on each Thursday night in June,
The day and month I died,
I promenade the Chapel yard,
I'm led by an unseen guide.

I'm waiting, and I'm waiting, and
Some night, 'tween one and nine,
There's sure to come, unthinkingly,
A man with head like mine.

I'll charm him with a magic spell
I'll make him stand and stare.
And then I'll steal his head away
And leave him lying there.

And he will then rove 'round at night
As I, without a head;
While I shall fly far, far away
To live with the happy dead.

BOO!

The End

CPSIA information can be obtained
at www.ICGtesting.com
Printed in the USA
BVOW09s2115290118
506622BV00002BA/274/P